BOOK
DRIVE

BOOK DRIVE

A NOVEL

ROBERT ERINGER

Bartleby Press
Washington • Baltimore

ISBN 978-0-935437-59-1

Library of Congress Control Number: 2021930867

Bartleby Press

PO Box 858
Savage, Maryland 20763
800-953-9929
www.BartlebythePublisher.com

Printed in the United States of America

10 9 8 7 6 5 4 3 2 1

In Memory of Claire DeSapio Gesualdi

PART ONE

1.

HERE it goes.

I'm going to tell you a story.

It is about a once-famous novelist named Christopher Lathom.

Visualize him: Lathom is about normal height and normal width disrupted by a paunch and a wrinkly, sun-dried countenance illustrative of his age, nearing seven decades. He dresses in black shirt and slacks, a well-worn Beretta olive safari vest and is never without a gray straw fedora to conceal his balding pate.

Lathom has an image to uphold, albeit mostly to himself due to his minimal social circulation.

His face sports a trim gray beard and moustache, a tad longer at the chin; crooked, yellowed teeth that reflect an absence of attention or regular check-ups (partly due to the expense, partly due to an abhorrence of medical practitioners, especially dentists).

In his mind, Lathom remains the famous author he once was thirty years earlier with the publication of *King Zero*—a novel critically acclaimed by all the influential book journals of the day and short-listed for several of the literary world's most prestigious prizes.

And thus, Lathom is elated to have finally completed, and readied for publication, his first novel since his debut: *Day of the Rabbits*, a tome of 690 pages—a length almost unheard of in book publishing as the world enters the twenty-first century's third decade.

Over time, while writing this magnum opus, the generous advance from Mulberry Press, his publisher, had long disappeared. To sustain himself, Lathom had sold his archives to a large university to support his writing habit—funds very nearly drained.

He could have taught English Lit at any college of his choosing, but our author disdained such a notion, believing that real writers don't teach, they write, financial survival be damned.

So, no surprise that Lathom lives a Spartan existence: a one bedroom condo in a rental unit on Coast Village Road, the main thoroughfare of a verdant and very precious community tucked between mountains and ocean along a bucolic strip of California coastline known as The American Riviera.

Location, location, location.

Hemingway, an early hero to Lathom, had his Key West, Havana and Ketchum, Idaho.

Hunter Thompson, whom he once knew, had his Woody Creek, Colorado.

Jim Harrison, an old drinking buddy, had his Patagonia, Arizona casita.

Lathom has Montecito, a tony enclave of multimillion dollar estates populated by Hollywood celebrities and Silicon Valley titans, along with the flimflammers that magnetically fixate and prey on the ultra-rich—and where even the publisher of the weekly gossip and real estate community rag keeps a dark pornographic secret.

This is where we find Chris Lathom, literary author, on the advent of his new masterpiece, studying the poster purporting to publicize his work, as designed by the marketing wizards of Mulberry, a respected literary imprint of one of New York's media behemoths.

True, the book's cover turned out to Lathom's liking, mostly because it boldly highlights his name featured more prominently than the abstract image.

But the verbiage contrived by copywriters was, in his learned opinion, amateurish; it is over such drivel he fumes while feeding lettuce to his sole companion, a pet bearded dragon named Scallywag.

2.

ON this warm mid-autumn morning, as with most mornings, Lathom departs his condo complex on foot for coffee.

Lathom does not drive, had not driven in years, partly due to the expense of owning and running a car and partly because his needs—outside of holing up at the old pine table he uses for writing, and reading the twaddle now before his eyes—are mostly within walking distance, through which he derives daily exercise.

Minutes later, trudging past plate-glass windows of Starbucks, he scouts out the caffeine emporium's interior, hoping not to recognize or—in his mind—be recognized. Lathom has few friends and tries his best to avoid running into acquaintances, mostly *The Entitled*—to his thinking; the downside of an existence in Montecito, where pristine vintage cars, Botox babes and slender bods abound.

"Bitch-witches," he hisses under his breath when faced

with the platinum-blonde, coiffed-eyebrow coffee moms assembled within.

It was almost as if the folks who had become too obnoxious for Los Angeles had moved ninety miles north to this exclusive slice of natural beauty and abundance.

Our author is relieved to see no one he knows.

He enters and, taking no chances that he missed someone who might want to say *hey*, beelines for the queue of a dozen or so patrons. He stands in line, with mounting impatience, watching incredulously as an assortment of customers pay for coffee and croissants by scanning smart phones, which, to Lathom's eye, takes twice as long as using cash money.

When it is finally his turn, he says, indignantly, to the cashier, "Isn't paying with your phone supposed to *save* time, not waste it? Does it not defeat the purpose?"

The cashier, a cog in the system, smiles and shrugs, just says *I guess so*, a nice way of saying *so what?*

"Dumbing down time in America," Lathom adds. "I'll have a large drip coffee."

"Name?"

"Smith."

Lathom pays in cash and with coffee in hand, shoots off to a far corner. He sits with his back to the gabby coffee moms and semi-retired if still self-important Hollywood bozos responsible for the dumbest situation comedies ever produced on television.

"Chris?"

Lathom stiffens.

"That you, Chris?"

Lathom turns—and looks up to see Rodney towering over him.

"Oh, hi," says Lathom tersely.

Rodney drives in every morning from Goleta, ten miles east, to fixture himself at a string of Montecito coffee shops. He offers his hand to shake; Lathom responds with a closed fist for a fleeting knuckle tap.

"You think I got cooties?" squawks Rodney in his distinctive Brooklyn accent.

In fact, Lathom believes *everyone* has cooties, and shakes with no one, fearing an onslaught of germs.

"May I join ya?" asks Rodney, seating himself.

Lathom cringes and Rodney immediately fixates on his favorite appendage: a smart phone. The author knows it is only a matter of moments before Rodney will commence a show-and-tell on its screen of all those material things he would buy if only he had the dough, demanding "Look at this! Look that that!" while holding the phone six inches from Lathom's nose, another vehicle for germ delivery.

Lathom's own cell—not a smart device but a cheap flip phone—rumbles inside his pocket until he plucks it out, studies the screen and answers.

"Good morning, Christopher."

Meet Jason Downey, high-powered New York City literary agent, erudite, and somewhat pretentious, phoning from his office in Mid-town Manhattan.

"Good of you to answer," says Downey with a hint of sarcasm. "I expected to leave a message. Again."

"Yeah, well." Lathom glances at Rodney and whispers into his phone, "I needed the distraction. And I'm glad you called because I have something to talk to you about." He pauses. "Doesn't anyone know how to write simple English anymore?"

"What do you mean?"

"The PR copy for my book. It's dreadful. Reads like jabberwocky. Who gets assigned this task, monkeys?"

Downey chuckles. "Welcome to the world of modern publishing. I'm afraid promotional copywriting is not as thoughtful as a quarter-century ago. If you have any specific…"

"I don't. I do my job, writing literature, they should do theirs, jingoism—and do it with a style and panache their authors and book readers expect of them. Would you please ask the publisher to provide adult supervision for their copywriters? I require correct handling. My fans have been waiting a long time for my second novel and I don't want them to get the wrong idea about my story through bad copywriting and shoddy promotion."

"I'll shoot them an e-mail to convey your concern." Maybe he would or maybe he wouldn't. But Downey had long ago learned the craft of coddling his stable of authors, most especially this needy one.

"Thank you. And please copy me on it," adds Lathom, not fully trusting his agent to do as he asked. "Oh, I suppose you have your own reason for calling?" He shoots a look of irritation at Rodney, who had not drifted away to provide space for a private conversation, but instead—much worse—seems to be eavesdropping.

"I do," says Downey. "I just wanted to ensure that you're all set for your book tour."

A long pause ensues as Lathom's attention switches from Rodney's intrusiveness to his agent's unexpected and unlikely utterance.

"My *what?*"

"Your book tour."

Incredulous, Lathom rises and leaving Rodney behind, walks with his coffee through an open door onto the adjacent patio bathed in golden sunlight.

"What book tour?" he hisses.

"The book tour your publisher is sending you on."

"What? *Nobody* is sending *me* anywhere."

"But you have to do a book tour." Downey's tone is matter of fact.

"I don't have to do anything of the sort," replies Lathom.

"I'm afraid you must."

"What do you mean, I *must?*" Lathom can feel his pulse quickening, and his blood pressure—already too high—steadily rising.

"Why must I?"

"Because doing a book tour is in your publishing contract."

Lathom can hardly believe his ears. "My publishing contract says *what?*"

"It states that part of your obligation as the author is to promote your novel by undertaking a book tour."

"Who agreed to *that?*"

Downey waits a few beats to compose his own exasperation. "Didn't you read the contract?"

"Of course not," scoffs Lathom. "That's *your* job. I never asked you to help write my novel, did I? So, why would you ask me to negotiate a publishing contract? You never mentioned any book tour."

"Yes, I did."

"When was that?"

"When the publishing agreement first arrived. I went through all the author responsibilities, one by one."

"I don't remember that."

"I do. What I do *not* remember is you objecting to anything at the time. And I also assumed you would enjoy getting out there to meet your readers, otherwise you would have…"

"You *assumed?*" Lathom is by now bordering on clinical shock. "Are you nuts? I would *not* enjoy *getting out there* to meet *anyone*—and you should have known that. I loathe public appearances. And I loathe being around people. My writing speaks for itself. I'm a writer, not a salesman."

"I understand how you feel," says Downey, harnessing all the charm he can muster for full placation mode.

"I don't think you have any idea how I feel."

"Being the writer is simply not enough these days," says Downey, filling a new silence. "Authors have to help sell their books and publishers want their authors out there in the marketplace to help whip up enthusiasm, build a momentum."

"Not my problem."

"A personal appearance by the author to sign copies is what compels bookstores to order many more copies than they might otherwise and pushes booksellers to display your books prominently in their window and on tables near checkout counter for all to see—and purchase."

"Bookstores should want to do that with my new novel anyway."

"Of course, they should. But they may not."

"And why is that?"

"Because," says Downey, with some trepidation, "there is a whole new generation of readers who have never heard of you."

Lathom feels as if his face has been slapped. "It doesn't matter because I'm not going on any book tour."

"But you can't breach your contract."

"Fuck the contract."

"I'm not so sure you want to do that."

"Why not?"

"Because, per the contract, the second half of your advance is contingent upon you taking a book tour."

"What? Who agreed to *that*?"

"You did. I negotiated the contract. You signed it."

"I can't believe this. Call them. Tell them it was a mistake."

"I can call them, but they won't see it that way," says Downey. "They'll see at as a breach of contract and will probably react badly."

Lathom says nothing, his anger mounting.

Downey fills the silence. "Your book tour is fully scheduled and your books have already been shipped to all of the participating bookstores."

"Well, tell them to *un*-schedule it!" Lathom claps his flip-phone shut. He pulls his arm back, about to fling the phone, but comes to his senses, recalling the last time he did this resulted in having to ride the bus to Santa Barbara and purchase a new one.

His phone rings again.

"Should've thrown it," he mutters to himself before placing the phone to his ear.

"Hanging up on me won't help resolve this issue," says Downey sternly. "Do you want to receive the second part of your advance?"

"Of course, I do."

"Then please listen to me. I'm reasonably certain Mulberry will *not* pay what's due until after you honor your contractual obligations and take the book tour they've organized. And if you absolutely refuse, it will be six months—your first royalty statement—before we see any more money."

"I don't fucking believe this," Lathom fumes. "Where, may I ask, am I supposed to be touring to?"

"First stop is Book Soup in West Hollywood."

The venue, a prestigious independent bookstore, isn't bad, but...

"Car-mageddon?" says Lathom.

"Excuse me?"

"Los Angeles. I call it Car-mageddon. It means the end of the world by motor car. I fucking hate LA and all its goddam traffic!"

"Book Soup is a premier venue. I'm told it took a lot of persuasion to get you in there."

This offends Lathom. "That's ridiculous," he scoffs. "My novel is a major publishing event."

"Exactly." Downey attempts to stroke his client's hubris. "That's why you need to be there."

"And when is this supposed to happen exactly?"

"Hasn't the publicity department been in contact with you?"

"No."

"They told me they've left over a dozen messages on your phone laying out everything you need to know about the book tour but you never call them back."

Lathom says nothing, fully cognizant that he had failed to listen to multiple messages.

"Book Soup," says Downey, shuffling papers, "is tomorrow evening at seven o'clock."

"*Tomorrow?*"

"At seven."

"That ridiculous! How am I supposed to even *get there*? You know I don't drive!"

"That part's easy," says Downey, feeling as though he's finally making some headway. "A media escort from Mulberry will pick you up, drive you to Book Soup and drive you home." He pauses. "Your next event is the following evening at Tecolote in Montecito. The publisher thought you might like that, a way to invite all your friends."

Silence.

"You there?"

"The publisher thought I might like that?" Lathom explodes, appalled. "Are they out of their fucking minds?"

Lathom could count *all his friends* on one hand—not including his thumb.

"The idea is to move books, capitalize on friends and relatives."

"Yeah, they're out of their fucking minds. Two bookstores better be all."

"Uh, no."

"Where else?"

"After that, the tour begins in earnest. It will take you up the Pacific coast to Seattle."

Downey is smart enough to hold the phone twelve inches away from his ear as his client takes a long moment to digest the magnitude of this bombshell.

"I'm supposed to travel all the way up to fucking Seattle like a fucking snake oil salesman hawking my wares?!"

This time the esteemed author cannot help himself. Enraged, he heaves his flip-phone as hard as he can across Coast Village Road and watches in awe as it smacks the pavement and splinters into a dozen pieces.

3.

AFTER many hours fuming while walking his beat—a circuitous route that takes Lathom through a tunnel beneath Interstate 101, over train tracks to Channel Drive alongside Butterfly Beach, past the Biltmore Hotel, a neighborhood to the right he calls "Baja Montecito" a bridge across the freeway, and the full length of Coast Village Road to Montecito Mart and Vons supermarket to pick up a few food items for his daily sustenance—he resolves to remain steadfast in his refusal to go on a book tour, finances be damned. He simply would not depart from what he liked to call, if only to himself, his "vicinal" existence.

Lathom's mind races.

My writing speaks for itself, always has, always will, and I'll starve to death before I prostrate myself in public—what am I, a literary prostitute? No, I am one of America's finest and best-known writers.

These thoughts do not abate, but consume him, his ego in charge, as usual—and a grandiose one at that.

On his way home, walking past Starbucks again, Lathom encounters a homeless man sitting near the entrance.

"Got any change for coffee?" says the unkempt, bearded man squatting on the ground.

"Change?" Lathom scoffs. "*Change* won't buy you coffee in *this* joint."

"You're right," says the man. "What I really need is a drink. A stiff one."

"Now you're talking." Lathom chuckles, digging into his pocket. He peels a ten-dollar bill from his bankroll and hands it to the man. "I appreciate honesty. No man should ever be denied a drink."

And then, with his paper bag of groceries, Lathom heads home: a quiet space of shoe-boxy and soulless white-washed rooms devoid of life, aside from Scallywag, who most of the time remains inanimate and fixated upon a light affixed to the roof of his aquarium—which is to say, devoid of life.

There'd been a wife once, long ago; mostly forgotten.

Lathom usually drinks at home, alone, maybe a shot or two of Reposado tequila. But on this day, come sunset, he feels like celebrating his defiant stance on *not* doing a book tour. So out he goes—a rare evening occurrence—for a bar hop around Montecito's lower village. He almost dives into Cava for its extensive (and reasonably-priced) tequila selection but instead opts to continue on, thinking maybe he'll save this bar for a nightcap.

Our author crosses the road and pops his head through the backdoor of Honor Bar, doesn't like who he sees—the usual gaggle of gadflies, including Rodney and his smart phone—and continues on to Lucky's.

The bar in Lucky's looks safe. No one is likely to approach him, meaning. he may rejoice by himself, his favorite company, and so, amid black matte walls decorated with black-and-white photographs of long-deceased movie stars that reflect his dark and highly introverted state of mind, Lathom rumps his rear on a stool at the far end of the bar and orders a pint of IPA.

Not two minutes later, T.C. Boyle, the acclaimed writer of novels and short stories, happens along after tying his poodle to a post before entering.

Tall, lanky, red-haired Boyle, buoyant and boyish despite his years and sporting a black beret, greets Ezra the bartender and a couple of regulars before noticing Lathom down the bar. He saunters over to greet him.

"Congratulations on your new book!" says Boyle, ever enthusiastic for the success of other writers.

Lathom nods, pleased to see T.C., both a lively raconteur and a worthy drinking mate, perhaps the only such person in town, maybe the whole state.

"I'm glad to see you have an event at Tecolote," says Boyle. "My favorite little bookstore in the world."

Lathom shakes his head. "Not me."

"No?"

"I didn't even know anything about it until this morning.

"I'm not going."

"Boycotting your own book signing?" Boyle chuckles, already familiar with Lathom's reclusive nature and persona.

"I shouldn't have to be on display."

"I like to think I shouldn't have to be on display, either," says Boyle. "But I do. We all do. I have a whole routine now—it's fun."

"Doesn't sound fun to me," Lathom grumbles, looking away.

"Your book has been a long time in the making," says Boyle. "You deserve the spotlight."

Lathom vigorously shakes his head and locks eyeballs with Boyle. "The spotlight should be on my book, my writing, not me."

"The spotlight these days is on the book *and* you. This is something you should try to enjoy, not hide out from. You get to be the center of attention."

"That's precisely the problem," says Lathom. "I eschew *any* attention focused on me or my life in general. Taking a book tour would drive me out of my mind."

"Look at that as a good thing," retorts Boyle. "Sometimes people, especially artists, need to get out of their minds."

"I don't understand."

Boyle places both hands atop his head then spreads his arms out. "Surrender yourself to the journey."

"But what if nobody shows up?" whispers Lathom.

"Ah." Boyle shrugs. "We've all gone through that. Did you hear the story about when Vonnegut became famous with Slaughterhouse Five?"

Lathom shakes his head.

"His book tour took him through Indianapolis. You'd think there'd be a big turnout for Kurt in his own hometown, right? Wrong. Everywhere else, he packed them in. But in Indy, where his grandfather built all the landmark buildings, hardly anyone showed up—proving that no one is a prophet in their own land."

"I see no point setting myself up for that kind of humiliation."

"Look at it another way," says Boyle. "There's nothing wrong with a little humbling." Boyle's attention is flagged down the bar. "Hope to see you at Tecolote."

Lathom broods into his beer and when it comes to brooding, Lathom is king.

Out the corner of his eye, he catches a male figure walking through the door, looking straight at him—and then aiming at him, too, a determined stomp. Wearing a jacket and tie, the stranger appears a wee bit out of place in this paradise of blue jeans, polo shirts and fleece vests.

Here we go—a fan in want of an autograph?

Sure enough, much to the author's displeasure, the man stops abruptly in front of him with something in his hand—*a book to sign? God forbid.*

"Christopher Lathom?"

"Guilty as charged."

"Uh-huh. I got something for you." The predator hands a packet of paper to his prey. "You've been served."

Lathom lamely accepts the documents. "Served with what?"

But the process server, having completed his singular task, has already turned on his heel, departing as quickly as he'd arrived.

Lathom studies a "Complaint" filed against him in United States District Court, Central District of California.

Copyright infringement?

He can hardly believe his eyes.

How the hell did I infringe somebody's copyright? I'm not a plagiarist—everything I write is highly original.

Reading further, he discovers this is not about a piece of prose. It's about a photograph of himself on the Author's Page in his name on Amazon. To Lathom's thinking, it makes no sense. Not only was he unaware that he *had* an Author's Page, but he'd never placed a photograph of himself on any such page. Or anywhere. Nor had he ever heard of this plaintiff, one Heinrich Schmucker, a purported professional photographer who claimed to own the copyright of said photograph.

Yet here was a federal case, in black and white, ascribed in terse legalese: Christopher Lathom is hereby ordered by the Court to respond to this Complaint within twenty-one days.

4.

Alighting from the MTD bus in downtown Santa Barbara, Lathom's first stop is T-Mobile on Paseo Nuevo to replace his flip phone. He is disconcerted to discover that the model he'd destroyed had been discontinued, requiring him to learn how to navigate a newer more sophisticated model; he curses himself for not controlling his impulses.

Adding insult to injury, Lathom must suffer a thirty-minute wait for a sales assistant, which severely tests his patience and leaves the humbled Lathom scowling. But he gets it done, waiving insurance and other extras sales reps are schooled to sell, and his effort is rewarded (or punished) with the piling up of several new voicemails from his agent and a 212 number, doubtless, his publisher.

No time for him to hear messages, as the author's next stop is the law offices of Josh Goodwin, Esquire.

Goodwin had fine-tuned this client's messy divorce more

than a decade ago—years after his wife and Lathom had legally separated, and had managed to squeeze the author into his busy calendar on short notice for a quick look at the lawsuit filed against him.

Facing Lathom from across his cluttered desk, Goodwin studies the first page and whistles softly.

"Federal Court." Goodwin eyes his client over reading spectacles. "That means LA. And much stricter procedures than superior court." He flips through the document. "Do you know anything about the photo this plaintiff, Schmucker, is talking about?"

Lathom shakes his head in disgust. "I have no friggin' idea."

"So, this is some kind of legal shakedown."

"Is that not an oxymoron?"

Goodwin chuckles sourly. "Not the way our so-called *justice* system operates. It would probably behoove you to settle this quickly rather than retain a lawyer and let it drag on."

"What do you mean, *settle it?*" This truly puzzles Lathom. He cocks his head, thinking maybe he misheard.

"Go-away money."

"Pay my hard-earned money for them to drop it?" Lathom pulls a face. "Why? I didn't do anything wrong."

"I believe you." Goodwin sighs. "But you've just become forcibly engaged in the unmerciful world of jurisprudence. This Schmucker and his ambulance-chasing lawyer are counting on an easy roll-over so they can move on to their next victim, and it will likely be far less expensive to pay them off than fight them. I'll do some research on this attorney." He squints at the opening page. "He's based in Westlake. I'll bet his office initiates dozens of cases like this every year and rarely litigates—a boiler room operation."

"How can they get away with that?"

Goodwin chuckles. "You kidding? This shit happens all the time. In fact, this is why courts are so clogged up with cases." He shakes his head. "And since copyright infringement is a *federal* matter, it's more expensive to defend. Every time there's a hearing, your lawyer has to show up in Federal Court, downtown LA. That's a lot of billable hours in travel time alone—even for a lawyer who *lives* in LA." The lawyer fixes his gaze upon Lathom. "These bastards are banking on the idea that you won't stomach the legal cost. It comes down to a mathematical formula: how much you will pay them that is less than your lawyer will cost you."

Lathom shakes his head, exasperated. "Can't we just write to the judge and tell them this is just a set-up—or what did you say, a shakedown?"

Goodwin laughs. "That's cute—are you serious?"

"Why not?"

"For a start, the legal system doesn't work that way. The legal system exists, ultimately, to benefit the legal system. You can either settle this before the twenty-one days are up or you have no choice but to have a lawyer respond to the claim."

"What if I just ignore it?"

"Uh-huh. Pretend it never happened—right?"

"Right."

"Wrong. That's an outcome they'd *welcome*. I don't know if you've actually read through this lawsuit but they're suing you for $150,000."

"WHAT?"

"Their claim states that your copyright infringement was *willful*. Meaning, you *intentionally* violated this photographer's copyright full knowing his photo was copyrighted. If you ignore the Complaint, they'll move for a default judgment and get the whole amount awarded against you. Then they'll try to enforce the judgement by raiding your bank account…"

"There's not much in there…"

"…and go to your publisher with a court order to garnish your royalties."

Lathom can feel the blood drain from his face. "All right, all right. What should I do?"

"I could give them a call and see what they're willing to settle for, make them believe we'll fight if their settlement demand is unreasonable. They don't really want to prosecute this case because it's too much like real work. Hopefully, they'll take a few thousand and crawl back under a rock."

"A few thousand *dollars*?"

"That would be a good deal. A simple response to this Complaint will cost you a few thousand—and that's just the beginning."

"Okay, okay. Please call them, try to settle it."

"And I'll also try to identify a good IP lawyer in case you need to respond to the Complaint." He pauses. "You have a book coming out soon, don't you?"

"Today."

"Congratulations. It probably explains their timing."

"Huh?" Lathom tilts his head.

"One, it means they think you have some money, and two, they're betting you don't want any bad publicity."

Lathom groans. "I didn't think of that."

"Well, you can be certain *they* have."

"This is Anti-Aladdin's lamp," says Lathom.

"What's that?"

"The genie comes out of the bottle and you don't get any wishes. That's because this is the genie's evil twin brother. It arrives in a cloud of flatulence and gets to shit on you whenever it wants the rest of your life."

5.

TUCKED back inside his sparse apartment, Chris Lathom listens lugubriously to the voice mails that have piled up on his phone. They alternate between his agent and his publisher, each pleading and cajoling about a venue at Book Soup in Hollywood this very day, the official publication date of his long-awaited novel.

This he had been expecting.

What he did not expect was for his doorbell to ring—a seldom sound. Having been spooked the evening earlier— *could it be another process server?* —his inclination is to ignore it and hide.

But the situation soon escalates to a determined pounding on his door.

And then a new call from his agent, which Lathom answers as far from his door as possible. "Yes?"

"Are you home?" asks Jason Downey.

"Yes," says Lathom suspiciously. "Why are you asking?"

"I just got a call from the publisher to say that their media escort is at your door—would you please open it?"

"Why should I?"

"Because he's there to drive you to Book Soup in LA."

"I don't want to go to LA."

"It'll be a huge mistake if you don't."

"I thought you were going to tell them to cancel the tour?"

"I said I'd talk to them," says Downey. "And I did."

"And?"

"They didn't want to hear my message. They refused to budge."

"On what basis?"

"On the basis that you'll be in breach of your publishing contract if you don't show up for your book tour, starting with Book Soup this evening. I took some notes. Hold on."

"Jesus H. Christ," Lathom mutters.

"Okay, this was their response," Downey resumed. "*Not only will they hold up the advance, they'll also stop shipping books and focus their energies on other titles with more cooperative authors.* Their words, not mine."

"This is blackmail!"

"No, Chris, this is reality," says Downey. "And you need to get real. You need to open your door and get ready to be driven to LA. Just show up. You don't have to do a reading. Just show up, for chrissakes, sign a few books—that'll satisfy the terms of the contract. Meantime, I'll start working on getting your book tour shortened, maybe due to some kind of feigned illness or something."

Lathom disconnects without a goodbye and opens his door.

On his doorstep Lathom finds a scrawny kid with a fresh face, mopped with thick brown hair, barely out of college, impeccably dressed in Banana Republic smart casual: khaki trousers, white button-down shirt, unconstructed sportcoat—as if bespoke—and skinny tie anchored by burgundy penny loafers.

"Mister Lathom?" He looks at the author in awe. "I'm…"

"I know, I know. The goddamned media escort," he spits out, glowering. "How much time have I got?"

The young man checks his smart phone. "You never know with traffic, sir," he says, studying Lathom closely. "I think we should get going as soon as possible."

"Something wrong?" asks Lathom, discomfited by the eyeball lock.

The media escort looks down at his feet, shuffling them, avoiding the author's gaze. "You remind me a little of someone," he mumbles.

Lathom harrumphs, rolling his eyes. "Go to Starbucks." He hands the kid a ten-dollar bill. "Get us some coffee. Black for me, no sugar. I'll try to be ready by the time you get back."

6.

"By the way, my name is Blythe," says the media escort after Chris Lathom has ensconced himself comfortably in the backseat of a clean silver Ford Escape, paper cup of coffee in hand.

Lathom is dressed, as before, in a safari vest and a straw fedora. "Is that your first or last name?"

"Just call me Blythe."

"Okay, Just Blythe it is."

Blythe steers across the Olive Mill Road intersection and ramps onto Interstate 101, southbound.

"So, how long have you been doing this, *Just Blythe?*" asks Lathom.

"Escorting authors? You're only my second."

Lathom sips his coffee.

"Who was your first?"

"One of the Kardashians."

Lathom cringes. "Did the *real* writer join you for any of it?"

Blythe chuckles. "Media escorting has replaced the mailroom as an entry-level job in publishing. That's me, entry level."

"Uh-huh." Lathom is distracted by his own thoughts, the copyright infringement lawsuit, which clings to his mind like barnacles to the side of a barge.

"Actually, I'd like to be a writer," Blythe adds.

Lathom considers this. "Are you ignorant, Just Blythe? Or nuts?"

"What do you mean?"

"Why would anybody want to be a writer, or an artist, or a singer-songwriter, or want to do anything in the arts anymore?"

"Why not?"

"Because John Q. Public won't *pay* anymore, that's why not. They expect to be given anything artists create for *free* through the Internet. Which means artists, especially new artists, can no longer earn a living doing their art."

Blythe shrugs. "I just like to write."

"Okay, then write. But if you want to write well, start by getting out into the world and *live*. Without life experience, you won't have anything to write about. The more life experience, the likelier you'll have something good and true to write about."

"As in, write *what you know?*"

"*Write what you know, show don't tell, blah-blah-blah.*"

Lathom waves one arm around, flapping his hand. "You can read all the how-to books about writing you want, by people who teach but don't write. But the only way you'll ever get good at writing is to write, write, write, every day, and never stop. And when you're not writing, read. But only read *good* writing, because if you read *bad* writing, you'll *write* bad." He pauses. "Sonofabitch, I forgot my hand sanitizer. We're going to have to stop somewhere and buy a new one."

"No problem, Mister Lathom, we can do that. How old were you when you started to write?"

Lathom regards his driver suspiciously through the rear-view mirror. "You're not a reporter posing as a driver, are you?"

"No, sir. Just curious."

"Okay, then. Curiosity is good for a budding writer. But nothing I say had better end up in a newspaper or a magazine—or, God help us—a blog."

"No, sir."

"A writer needs curiosity. Lots of it. Truth is, some people are good at words, some are good at numbers, they're just born that way, right brain, left brain. And most people are nothing more than biological robots with feelings that get programmed into them, incapable of creative thought. That's why they're able to work nine-to-five jobs inside a giant shoebox beneath fluorescent light without wanting to kill themselves. But they might as well have never been born." Lathom glares out of his window. "I'd rather be homeless than live that kind of a non-life. And under fluorescent light? It steals your creativity, if you ever had any, and sucks all your energy dry. Trust me, you're better off doing what you're doing, driving a car as an escort, then working in some publishing office somewhere full of fluorescence, flatulence and hierarchy. Office politics." Lathom scoffs. "It's the same with every field, even the literary world, all populated with corrupt back-stabbers. I should have won a Pulitzer Prize for my last book—and would have, but for the snobs who populate literary politics." He shakes his head in disgust recalling the snob snub.

Lathom's phone sounds. He checks the caller's identity and answers.

"I spoke with the plaintiff's attorney," says Josh Goodwin, Esquire.

"And?"

"They say they want fifty-grand to settle it."

"Fifty thousand dollars? Are they out of their fucking minds? For one stupid photograph of *me*? I don't even *like* having my photograph taken—and especially not for dissemination to the public!"

"Copyright infringement is a serious issue," says Goodwin somewhat solemnly. "While it's true that copyright law pertaining to photography has become a ridiculous relic in this digital age of social media and instant imaging, until the laws get modernized and restructured the court has no choice but to respect the letter of the law. I couldn't talk him down. Which means we're going to have to file a Response to the Complaint."

"God damn it! Who is this plaintiff anyway?"

"Yes, I did a little research on this Schmucker guy. He's what's known in the legal world as a serial suer, which some people believe should be spelled s-e-w-e-r."

"A what?"

"Someone who sues a lot. He obviously can't make a living through photography—either because he's a third-rate photographer or because the times we live in have rendered his vocation irrelevant—so he makes whatever money he lives on by threatening to sue people for copyright infringement and shaking them down for a quick settlement so they can avoid expensive legal fees."

"How can he get away with a scheme like that?"

"Judges generally don't like serial plaintiffs. And sometimes they get declared vexatious litigants, which prohibits them from suing without special permission from the court. But because this Schmucker sticks to the letter of the law they have no choice but to allow him due process. Most of the time his victims pay him to go away. For every case that made it into court, there are probably a dozen who rolled over at the first sign of trouble. The lawyers who file on his behalf are no better. Scumbags, all of them, working on contingency, which means he doesn't have to pay anything, win or lose. The lawyer is in it for thirty percent of the kill."

"I get that. But how do they have a case against *me*?"

"You have an Author's Page on Amazon, right?"

"I guess. I don't pay attention to the Internet."

"Well, there's a photograph of you on that page."

"So what?"

"Did you put it there?"

"Of course not."

"Then how did it get there?"

"How the hell am I supposed to know?"

"Well, it's in your name. And there's a photo of you on the site that this photographer claims to have taken, which means he owns the rights to his intellectual property. And this plaintiff alleges that you willfully infringed his copyright by using his photograph without permission."

"But I don't even want it there! I don't like my picture taken and I do not want photos of me available to anyone. Hell, there isn't even a photo of me on the jacket of my new novel!"

"I believe you. Unscrupulous photographers take pictures and post them somewhere public. Then they troll the Internet hoping someone has *re*-posted them on social media, equating to unauthorized usage—and if they don't get an immediate pay-off, they threaten a lawsuit or just go ahead and file one."

"So, what should I do."

"Find a lawyer to represent you."

"You're a lawyer. You represent me."

"Not a good idea."

"Why not?"

"I don't know as much as I should about IP law and…"

"IP?"

"Intellectual property. You're up against sharks who specialize in it. The best I can do, as I told you when you visited my office, is make another call or two, see if I can find the right IP lawyer in LA to represent you."

"Isn't there anyone in Santa Barbara who could do it?"

"None that I know of. Maybe Ventura, I'll check."

Just past Woodland Hills, an LA valley suburb, thickening traffic slows to a standstill.

Lathom shakes his head in disgust.

"I knew it," he mutters.

"Knew what?" asks Blythe.

"Car-mageddon." He twists his neck this way and that. "This isn't a road, it's a freakin' parking lot."

"Uh-huh," says Blythe blandly. "That's why I recommended an early start. According to my phone-map we should arrive right on time."

7.

THE window display of Book Soup on Sunset Boulevard is chock-a-block with hardcover copies of Day of the Rabbits by Christopher Lathom, along with a large poster announcing his gig.

The only thing missing is people.

Lathom stands at the doorframe, peering inside at rows and rows of empty wooden chairs facing a lectern.

He is still standing, ashen-faced, incredulous and unwilling to enter the barren shop, when Blythe returns from a parking lot nearby.

Lathom gestures with a scowl at the quietude inside. "There's nobody here."

"We're fifteen minutes early," says Blythe. "C'mon—let's go in, see what's happening."

Inside, the bookstore manager does not recognize Lathom.

When Blythe whispers into her ear that their guest author has arrived, she greets him effusively.

"It is such an honor to have you here." She pauses. "I'm so sorry about the review in *Kirkus*."

"Huh?" says Lathom. "What review?"

"I thought it was very unkind," she adds, shaking her head sympathetically.

"I haven't seen it." Lathom considers whether or not he really wants to see it, given her reaction. But curiosity gets the better of him, his rancor rising. "Do you have a copy here?"

"Of course." She moves off, still shaking her head. "This way. So very, very unfair."

Lathom grimaces in abhorrence of being pitied and follows her to the checkout-counter, on which sits a stack of *Kirkus Reviews*, delivered that day, along with a smattering of other book publishing periodicals.

Tucked way back on page eight—much too far back for his liking—is a review entitled "Bad Day for Rabbits."

Lathom winces.

The piece begins with a question: *This is what took the erstwhile Christopher Lathom a quarter-century to write?*

Whatever blood is left in Lathom's face drains as he reads the review in its entirety, finally taking a seat to steady his nerves—and his nerves certainly need steadying when he reaches a line, near the end, that states, *Mr. Lathom is clearly a has-been who need not reapply to 'still is' status.*

The piece concludes by depicting the author's lengthy work as *an exercise in logorrhea.*

Lathom yanks his phone from a pocket and, trembling with anger, connects to his agent.

"Are you at Book Soup?" Downey answers with an anxious question.

"Never mind that—have you seen *Kirkus?*"

A long pause ensues before Downey finally speaks. "Yes, it only just came out today."

"Who the fuck is behind this?" demands Lathom. "It's that same little clique of literary shits I had to contend with decades ago, isn't it? And people wonder why Salinger never published again! This is an abomination!"

"Sticks and stones," says Downey, trying to quell his client's tantrum. "At least they published a review."

"Excuse me? You call this a review? This is *not* a re-view—it's a *hatchet job!* Ordered up and delivered to my literary enemies!"

"Please tell me you're at Book Soup."

"I'm here." Lathom glances around the near-empty store. "But no one else is."

"What do you mean?"

"Simple English. There's *no one here!*"

"No one?"

In fact, two persons had walked in and taken seats two minutes before show time.

"Unbelievable," Lathom mutters before disconnecting.

"We're ready for you, Mr. Lathom," says the bookstore manager, guiding him with a gentle tug on his elbow, to the lectern.

Another three persons who had been browsing book-shelves have also taken seats, creating an audience of seven, including Blythe and the store manager. As she runs through her laudatory if brief introduction, Lathom looks at his smattering of an audience in abject disbelief.

And then she turns it over to him.

"I've already said what I needed to say in my book," Lathom announces to the tidy group. "I'm a writer, not a speaker, and if I had anything else on my mind it would have been *written* in the book, not *spoken* here."

He pauses. "But I'll answer a few questions," adding under his breath, "if I must."

A studious young woman with short black hair and glasses raises her hand. "What does the title mean?"

Lathom barely opens his tightened lips. "I suggest you read the book," he says curtly. "That is customarily how meaning is derived from a title."

Embarrassed, the woman stands and quickly departs, on her way out passing a new arrival who is wearing a vest much like Lathom's own, though this one pockets bulge with lenses and other camera accoutrements. The new arrival, a middle-aged male, raises and points a large camera at Lathom.

The author responds by turning his back on the photographer, a general dislike of having his picture taken exacerbated by his recent brush with a copyright lawsuit from a photographer.

"No photos!" he hisses to the bookstore manager, sitting a couple yards away in the front row. "Didn't the publisher tell you that?"

"Why, no," says the bewildered manager.

She reluctantly rises and works her way over to the photographer who, in any case, has already got what he needs, and skedaddles out the door before she can say boo.

Not fifteen minutes after it began, the manager initiates a round of applause—tepid, at best—and invites the audience to visit the cashier to purchase signed copies.

An older gentleman approaches Lathom to request a signature on his first book from decades ago.

"No." Lathom waves him away. "You'd probably put it on eBay."

Lathom's germ phobia is nothing compared to his phobia of being taken advantage of by other people.

He turns and scoots out the door, briskly setting off on foot in an easterly direction down Sunset Boulevard, leaving *Just Blythe* the media escort in hot pursuit.

8.

THE night is fresh and alive, the neighborhood a swirl of colorful illumination as Lathom rapidly traverses a stretch once the trendiest in Hollywood—Dino's, 77 Sunset Strip, long gone. He fills his lungs with cool air, feeling free and even ecstatic for a few brief moments before catching himself to wonder why he should feel so good given the pathetic turnout for him at Book Soup and a terrible review in *Kirkus*, negative thoughts that immediately bring him back down to dark bitterness where he's more at home.

After hoofing it a mile, he decides where he must go. It takes another twenty minutes to reach this destination: Musso & Frank Grill, as musty and musky inside as the old-timers who have served this venerable "genesis of Hollywood" and its regular patrons so faithfully for over half-a-century.

Upon arriving, and rumping his rear onto a barstool, the author demands his just reward: a vodka martini with three olives. A serious pour from a serious bartender, who provides a sidecar to keep the spillover icy cold.

Within a minute Blythe reappears, out of breath. He takes the stool next to Lathom.

"Jeez, if I'd known you were coming all this way I'd have driven."

Lathom shrugs. "I didn't know it myself until inspiration struck. Cheers." He toasts the air and moistens his lips with liquid crystal, then closes one eye and squints the other at his media escort. "Are you even old enough to drink?"

"I'm twenty-two."

"That's a relief." Lathom raises his forefinger. "Bartender!"

"But I can't," says Blythe. "I'm driving."

"C'mon, you're allowed one drink."

Blythe eyes Lathom's oversized martini-with-sidecar. "One of those is like three anywhere else. Anyway, I'm working, it's against company policy."

"I have an aphorism for that," says Lathom. "Company policies deserve to be broken." He takes a gulp of ice-cold vodka. "At least loosen your goddam tie."

Blythe does as he's told while Lathom glances around at the ghosts he feels nearby. "John Fante used to drink four of these babies and drive all the way home to Point Dume in Malibu," he says. "Faulkner, too, with his buddy, Stephen Longstreet, who brought him to Hollywood for his screenwriting phase. And F. Scott. He lived nearby—a lightweight drinker. This place was a true writer's watering hole." He shakes his head. "Those were the days."

"Did you hang out with any of them?"

Lathom studies Blythe with incredulity. "How old do I look to you?"

Blythe's cell rings. He answers, glances at Lathom, saunters from the bar to the back room to talk in private, returns a few minutes later.

"Was that *them*?" asks Lathom.

'Who?"

"You know who I mean. The suits at Mulberry."

"Uh, yeah, my boss wanted to know how it went."

"Did you happen to mention to him that we had them lining up around the corner?"

Blythe does not reply.

"Or about the rave review in Kirkus?"

"My boss is a *she*. She already knows about the review. And she's not happy about it."

"*She's* not happy about it? Did she happen to ask how *I* feel? Or mention what *she's* planning to *do* about it?"

Blythe shakes his head. "I'm just a lowly media escort."

"So, what *did* she say?"

"She wants me to make sure I get you home at a reasonable hour tonight so that you're fresh for your book event in Montecito tomorrow evening. *Drink up*. Her words, not mine."

Lathom almost chokes on his gin. "Drink up? Women have taken over publishing, just like everything else, and the only thing they give a fuck about is publishing books by transgender Chinese. Drink up. Yeah, right. This is really about the new wave of female publishing executives trying to orchestrate the emasculation of male authors, including myself. *Especially* myself." He shakes his head. "Yeah, let's embarrass the old white guy—America's new trend. Reverse discrimination, politically correct bigotry, perpetrated by ethnicities, feminists, transgender gays and self-loathing white guys. Let me tell you something, if women didn't have a snatch there'd be a bounty on them."

"I'm guessing you're not a huge fan of marriage," says Blythe.

"Let me tell you about marriage," says Lathom. "A wedding license should be good for seven years only—and renewable only by *mutual* consent."

"Did yours end that way?"

"Oh, yeah—it was definitely mutual. But it cost me almost everything I owned to renew my life. Cured me of marriage forever." Lathom drains his martini glass. "Bartender! Give me another. Exactly the same!"

"You sure?" says Blythe. "My boss wasn't too happy when I told her where we are."

"Aww. Not too happy, is she? What a shame." Lathom pops an olive into his mouth. Dinner. "All the more reason I'm staying for another cocktail. Women don't tell me what to do. Never have, never will."

9.

When Lathom awakens in his condo the next morning, he's not at all sure how he got there. His head feels as if a bomb detonated inside his skull; his mouth tastes like a trash can and his eyeballs are begging to be yanked out and run under cold water. His last memory: ordering a third martini and not eating dinner, having lost his appetite stressing over the lawsuit filed against him, further aggravated by a humiliating "event" at Book Soup, an evisceration from *Kirkus* and attempted emasculation by his publisher's marketing chief.

For coffee, this morning, he ambles east to Honor Bar, even if it means contending with Neanderthals— or more formally, in Lathom's lingo, The Neanderthal Coffee Club, which convenes around bistro tables on the open-air patio mid-morning until the assembled male complainants, mostly displaced New Yorkers, get chased off at 10:55 to make way for more serious spenders, the lunch patrons.

From his own table, Lathom overhears the incessant Neanderthal gripes, groans and whines, ironic to the author's ears because their bellyaching is set in a region of abundance and temperate climate.

This does nothing to quell his massive hangover, rendered all the worse by a missed call from his agent—*ignore the sonofabitch*—and a voicemail from his lawyer, unpleasantly reminding him of his strange new entrée into the world of copyright infringement and jurisprudence.

Lathom's thoughts, blacker than the coffee in his cup, are soon interrupted.

"Ya gonna join us or what?" squawks Rodney from the Neanderthal camp.

"If I want whine," scoffs Lathom, "I uncork a bottle."

"Sorry about your event at Tecolote tonight," says Rodney.

"Huh—what do you mean, *sorry?*"

"Haven't you heard?"

"Heard what?"

"Evacuation order, four p.m. today—a nasty rainstorm blowing in. Everything has to close up tight. Too bad, because we were all planning to show up and cheer you on."

Such a notion leaves Lathom harrumphing.

10.

Upon returning home, Lathom finds *Just Blythe* on his doorstep.

"Not you again," he says.

"Yes, me."

"Haven't you heard, *Just Blythe*?" says Lathom. "You can go home because tonight's event is cancelled. Mother Nature is in charge, as always, and Montecito's entitled are fleeing her reproach."

"Yeah, but there's still the book tour," says Blythe. "You're expected in Healdsburg tomorrow evening."

"Ha!" Lathom bristles. "After that debacle in LA? I don't think so."

"But it's all arranged. My instructions from Mulberry are to drive you to Healdsburg."

"What you mean is, you've been instructed to *kidnap* me," snarls Lathom, shaking his head. "I don't think so. My agent told Mulberry I'm not going. At least that's what he was *supposed* to tell them." Lathom pauses. "And, by the way, if I were really going to the Bay area on a book tour, it should have been to City Lights in North Beach, not some one-horse town further north."

Blythe consults his itinerary. "That's not what it says here."

"What *does* it say?"

"Copperfield's, Healdsburg. After that, Ashland, Oregon, then Portland and..."

"Powell's?"

"Huh?"

"Powell's. In Portland. The largest bookstore in the country."

Blythe squints at the document. "It doesn't say *Powell's*. It says New Renaissance Books."

Lathom shakes his head in dismay. "What the hell kind of cockamamie book tour is this supposed to be, anyway? No City Lights, no Powell's, no fucking way! You're excused, *Just Blythe*. Tell the suits at Mulberry to shove their freakin' book tour as far the hell up their colon as it will go." He rubs his head. "And by the way, how the hell did I get home last night?"

"I drove you."

"Oh."

"I'm staying at the Coast Village Inn up the road. We should depart no later than ten tomorrow morning."

"I just told you!" Lathom explodes, exasperated. "Don't you get it? I'm not going anywhere!"

Blythe hands Lathom a card. "Here's my number if you change your mind. My orders are to remain in Montecito and drive you on a book tour. I'm not allowed to leave without you."

And off goes *Just Blythe*.

Still feeling sick to his stomach, Lathom prostrates himself onto his sofa and listens to Josh Goodwin's voicemail recommending an intellectual property specialist in Ventura with a direct cell number, which Lathom calls.

"Ah, yes," says Glenn Pioche. "Josh faxed me the Complaint and told me about his conversation with Plaintiff's counsel. I can have my own chat with him, see if they're willing to negotiate and, if not, prepare a Reply to the Court if you want to retain me."

"I don't think I have much choice."

"In that case, I'll prepare a Retainer letter. It will need your signature, you can do it by DocuSign."

"What the hell is DocuSign?"

Pioche chuckles. "Don't worry, I'll walk you through it. Oh, and I'll need five thousand dollars to get started."

"Five thousand dollars?" Lathom's stomach somersaults.

"That'll get us through the first hurdle or two."

"The first hurdle or two? How much is this going to cost me *total?*"

"Hard to say," says Pioche. "Once they see we're serious about defending you against baseless allegations, they'll probably lower their demand, which is what I'm angling for. But if they want to get into discovery, well, that would probably cost another five-grand, at least, depending on how much there is to discover. Next, depositions, maybe another five-grand to depose the plaintiff and yourself."

"I'll have to sit for a deposition?"

"If it goes that far. After discovery, court-ordered mediation, where most cases are resolved. Another five-grand…"

Lathom erupts. "How many friggin' five grands are there?"

"Depends how long it goes on. And if it goes to trial, figure *twenty*-five grand."

Reeling from this onslaught of multiples, Lathom next calls his agent.

"I've been trying to reach you," says Jason Downey. "How are you?"

"Unruly."

"But of course. How was Book Soup?"

"I already told you! Book Soup was a *non*-event! Nobody was there! It wasn't worth the gas money it took to get me there and back!"

"You mean it never picked up after we spoke?"

"No!" Lathom holds out his phone as if it were a disease. "Didn't Mulberry Press bother to advertise it?"

"I'm certain they did. As far as I know their publicity department is on it."

"Oh, really? Well, despite what you know, they seem *off* it to me. I think they sold three books."

"That bad?"

"Worse than bad. Please tell me Mulberry has agreed to cancel the book tour."

Downey hesitates briefly before responding. "I'm sorry, but

I can't tell you that because they haven't. On the contrary, they're quite insistent that the book tour should go ahead as scheduled."

"Even after the Book Soup debacle?"

"Yes. I spoke with their head of publicity this morning. She's a real piece of work, won't budge an inch. She pointed out that because you did a signing at Book Soup the store will continue to display the books in their window until their next author event. Same with the other booksellers on the tour. It means larger orders than otherwise and prominent displays. And that, she says, increases sales."

"But they couldn't even get me into Powell's for chrissakes! Has the world gone to hell in a handbasket?"

Downey gives this serious consideration. "In fact," he finally says, "the world *has* gone to hell in a handbasket—for book publishers, anyway."

"I don't get it."

"I'll try to explain." He pauses to gather his thoughts into a succinct analysis. "Book publishing is officially a dinosaur—with extinction visible on the horizon. Publishers are doing everything they can within their power just to remain solvent. I know it's difficult for you, but please find it in your heart just to be grateful that Mulberry is even giving you a book tour—or any attention at all. These days most of their marketing resources are spent on Hollywood celebrity books and famous authors."

"I'm not famous?"

Downey skillfully evades the question, choosing his words carefully. "Mulberry says it's all arranged, you can't cancel."

"And if I simply don't go?"

"If you boycott the tour, Mulberry they will withhold the second half of your advance."

"So, we'll sue them for it, right?"

"That would not be prudent. The courts are so back-logged, by the time it gets before a judge you'll already have your first six-month royalty check, from which the advance derives. And that's aside from the fact that you'd probably lose due to breach of contract."

"Thanks to you."

"Be it as it may," says Downey, not wishing to engage in a pissing match. "If you don't go, which I don't recommend, the best I can do is write Mulberry a stern letter suggesting they will next hear from your lawyer. But they would probably ignore it unless and until they actually *hear* from your lawyer and, meanwhile, threatening a lawsuit against them would garner bad feeling among the team at Mulberry working to promote your book. You need them on your side, especially now, in light of a bad *Kirkus* review."

"That is a travesty! I'm never publishing again!"

"In that case, you'd better earn as much money from this title as you possibly can, starting with getting the rest of the advance due to you ASAP."

Lathom changes gears. "Why hasn't the New York Times reviewed my book yet?"

Another long pause ensues. "I spoke with the Times Book Review section yesterday," says Downey. "They told me they'd been planning a review this Sunday…"

"Good."

"No, not good. They decided against it."

"What do you mean, *decided against it?*"

"They won't explain their reasoning to me or Mulberry other than their procedure for selection is proprietary."

"What the hell does that mean?"

"Proprietary means…"

"I know what proprietary means! I'm a man of letters, for chrissakes, with a huge command of the language! But what I don't know is why they're spewing such nonsense! My novel has been anticipated for years!"

"It was politely suggested they gave up waiting a long time ago. Personally, I think the review in *Kirkus* put them off—at least for a week or two. You want my advice? Take the book tour. It might help rebuild momentum—and bring them back into the fold."

"Beg for their attention? Not happening! To hell with Mulberry and those peck-sniff literary snots at the Times!"

Feeling the red-hot lava within him about to erupt, Lathom drops his phone to the floor to prevent himself from throwing it over the balcony.

***

Near four o'clock in the afternoon, Coast Village Road fills with police cruisers as Santa Barbara sheriff's deputies commence the process of prodding several thousand of Montecito's inhabitants to evacuate their homes, and to ensure that the shops and restaurants on most of this main thoroughfare are locking their doors to business due to violent rainstorms forecast to blow in from the wine valley, other side of the Santa Ynez Mountains.

11.

Round about two in the morning, a restless Lathom lies in bed listening to the wind and rain lashing against his windows, reminding him of the monsoons he once experienced as a rookie reporter in Vietnam so very long ago. Perhaps his nihilistic bent derives from that dark experience.

Later, upon awakening at dawn, he hits a light switch and discovers he has no power. And no flashlight, either. So, without bothering to brush his teeth in the pitch-dark bathroom, he dresses quickly and descends to his morning ritual, only to find, due to utter turmoil along Coast Village Road, that his morning ritual no longer exists.

The ferocious rainstorm had, a couple hours earlier, induced a catastrophic mudslide and debris flow from Montecito Peak down through two main creeks and assorted roadways all the way to the ocean. These eight-foot high rivers of mud, filled with boulders, trees, cars and parts of houses, had formed multiple tributaries that flooded the lower village.

Lathom looks around in shock and awe as fire department crewmen stand around scratching their heads, also in awe, mostly by the mammoth clean-up that will likely take many weeks, probably months, perhaps even years, to bring things back the way they used to be.

In addition, mud had buried a tranche of Interstate 101 at Olive Mill Road, closing this vital artery in both directions, indefinitely, and quite likely for weeks, not days.

Lathom takes it all in. And there is quite a lot to absorb, a surreal mess; fire rescue vehicles parked haphazardly here and there manned by exhausted first responders. He overhears people talking about reports of over a hundred houses taken out by Mother Nature—and perhaps hundreds of millions of dollars in damage.

And then there is the vile stench. An odor not like anything else Lathom had ever smelled, leaving him with an urge to retch.

It was as if the devil itself had farted and pooped all over this piece of paradise.

Lathom quite rightly assesses that his natural habitat has been seriously disrupted, leaving any kind of normalcy impossible. Especially without a set of wheels.

And then, to top it off, sheriff's deputies show up at his Villa Fontana complex and demand, due to a clear and present danger, that all residents evacuate, effective immediately. This is due to widespread gas leaks, they not so calmly explain because one such leak had already caused a deadly explosion. Natural gas has therefore been occluded at source, with no plan to switch it back on anytime soon. Add to that a badly broken and corrupted water distribution system, leaving tap water unfit to bathe in let alone drink—and with no power, absent of means to boil it.

As his neighbors pack up their cars around him, most aiming for expensive Santa Barbara hotels or the homes of friends, Lathom clicks to the notion of an all-expense-paid exit ramp already constructed for him. It is not only the least expensive way to get through this inconvenience, but he'll also be able to collect the advance due him without a fight—*and* have the bread needed to pay Glenn Pioche to commence defending himself from copyright infringement—at least enough to insulate himself from a default judgment.

Lathom taps out the number on *Just Blythe's* business card. "Ready to roll, kid?"

12.

BLYTHE is as shell-shocked as everyone else as the magnitude of damages, injuries missing persons and confirmed fatalities become known and gossiped about by those hurriedly departing the darkened Coast Village Inn, along with word that the only road going south to the City of Angels no longer exists, and the alternative, around the mountains, takes over five hours instead of the usual two.

He hastily packs and makes his way to Lathom's condo.

"Come on in," says Lathom to Blythe. "You need to help me with Scallywag."

"With what?"

"Not a what, a *who*."

Blythe follows Lathom into the living room, to a console against a wall on which sits a glass aquarium with a large scaly trance-like lizard inside.

"That?" asks a puzzled Blythe.

"Scallywag is not a *what* or a *that*," says Lathom. "He's a bearded dragon. And he can't remain here. The power's out, so no heat lamp. How long are we supposed to be on this hayride to doom, anyway?"

Blythe hisses, a hush of a hiss, almost as if he were a bearded dragon himself and consults his itinerary. "One week."

Lathom looks to the sky. "God help us," he groans. "But that settles it. Scallywag's definitely joining us."

Just before departing the apartment, Lathom tries to check his e-mail to see if the retainer letter from Glenn Pioche and his demand for five grand to get cranked up has arrived, but, like everything else, the Internet is down, down, down.

Next, he calls his agent, Downey. Though cell service is patchy, very patchy, Lathom manages, on his third try, to at least leave him a voicemail:

"Okay, Mulberry wins. Surf's down, I'm off and running, face my readers, or no readers, take my lumps and afterwards go into exile like Salinger. Just tell them to send the advance check, pronto."

PART TWO

13.

AND so, the journey Christopher Lathom had tried his damndest to refuse now begins in earnest; a challenge reluctantly accepted, his own decision, albeit greased along by Mother Nature at her most devilish.

Blythe makes a right turn onto a chaotically congested Coast Village Road—and his vehicle immediately becomes embedded in mud, unwilling to budge further.

He studies his passenger.

"Don't look at me," says Lathom, shaking his head vigorously "*I'm* not getting out into this shit."

Blythe thrusts into reverse gear, which loosens the tires just enough to find a grip; a quick gear change lurches them forward and off they go, slowly passing Starbucks, which is, along with everything else, as Lathom puts it, "Shut tighter than a debutante on the cathedral steps."

They circle the roundabout halfway and veer onto 101

North, leaving the horror that has consumed Montecito this ghastly night in the dust, or rather, in the mud.

Rainclouds have abated by now and, in contrast, the sun shines serenely, adding to the surreal-ness of the natural disaster that had just occurred, as if the catastrophic event of a few hours earlier had never happened and a schizoid Mother Nature is smiling again.

Lathom is quiet, unsettled.

"How are you feeling?" asks Blythe.

"Unruly."

Blythe slips a CD into the player.

> *Get up, get up, get out of bed.*
> *And let the sunshine fill your head.*

Lathom opens his eyes briefly. "Sounds familiar. James Taylor?"

"No," says Blythe. "His younger brother, Livingston. This was his 1971 debut album. My grandmother used to play it."

Lathom grunts.

"She told me she thought Livingston's talent as a song-writer and performer got unfairly overshadowed by sweet baby James."

The interstate hugs the coast, beyond Santa Barbara, past the airport exit, through the built-up suburban sprawl in Goleta, then careens through hilly patches mostly brown or charred due to recent fires in the middle of a long drought that had been drying everything into tinder for five years—a condition abruptly ended by last night's torrential rainstorm.

The highway curves to the right, through Gaviota State

Park, a canyon that opens onto a flat landscape with open space and big sky.

They whiz past exits leading into urban Buellton and, just beyond, Los Olivos, an old stagecoach town brought back to life by vineyards and wine tasting emporiums. Further on are forbidding hillsides where the real Zorro and his confederates hid from armies sent by corrupt Mexican politicians to hunt them down.

Seeing cattle peacefully grazing in a hilly field, Blythe moos.

After the third such *moo*, Lathom eyes Blythe with suspicion and asks him what his problem is.

"I'm on the spectrum." says Blythe, somewhere between sheepish and cowed.

"The spectrum?"

"OCD."

"Ah, isn't everyone these days," says a disdainful Lathom. "What does that have to do with mooing at cows?"

"Everything. Part of my disorder is aboiment."

"A-boy-what?"

"Ever since I was a kid I make animal sounds—usually when I see an animal."

"Why?"

"I don't know *why*, I just do it. I can't help myself—it's involuntary."

"So, if you see a dog, you bark?"

Blythe nods. "Or growl."

"That's nuts."

Blythe shrugs. "Thank you for reminding me. I've learned to live with hearing it described that way. My therapist told me some people stutter, but something in my brain makes me blurt out animal sounds relating to whatever animal I see. It's a minor Tourette symptom, also known as echolalia."

"Echolalia," Lathom echoes. "So, what if you see a *picture* of an animal?"

"Sometimes that's all it takes. It depends how real the picture looks, I guess."

"You must be the life of the party at a zoo."

"Never been," says Blythe, cringing at the thought. "*Moooo!*" he rips a long one after another hillside dotted with longhorn steers gazing and grazing comes into view.

"You know what I call it?" says Lathom.

Blythe braces himself, having already heard everyone's theories for years.

"*Mindfluenza.* Unfortunately, your generation is almost wholly afflicted." Lathom chuckles. "They're going to need a whole new set of vaccinations for millennials, all to do with mental diseases." He brightens with a new realization. "Or maybe it's because the state pushed multiple vaccinations on all of you when you were toddlers without considering potential side effects down the road."

At Pismo Beach, they meet the coast again—a last look at a stretch of glistening blue ocean underscored by Avila's hillside of colorful cottages, before veering inland, this time for keeps.

"Watch for the Madonna Road exit, coming up," says

Lathom. "The Madonna is a savior for those who need to drain the snake."

Blythe shoots his passenger a puzzled look.

"No kidding. Best men's room in the State of California."

Blythe ramps to the right, cuts left, and right again into this colorful extravaganza of a landmark hotel, restaurant—and a rather decadent confectionery.

14.

BLYTHE IS waiting patiently behind the wheel when Lathom exits the Madonna Inn and climbs into the front seat.

"How did you come to be named Blythe?" he asks.

"It gets worse," says Blythe.

"How worse?"

"I'm from Blythe."

"Blythe, Arizona?"

"There's only one."

"Oh, c'mon," says Lathom, eyes flashing with incredulity.

"Blythe from Blythe?"

His driver nods.

"That's ridiculous and can't be true." The author's eyes narrow. "Are you putting me on?"

Blythe shrugs. "You asked, I'm telling you. I grew up in Blythe."

"Your name must have gone down well in elementary school."

"You had to be there." Blythe shakes his head mournfully. "You have no idea."

"I'd bet that's why you cultivated *mindfluenza*."

"Gee, Mister Lathom, you must have majored in psychology."

This is delivered with sweetness, not sarcasm.

"Don't be sassy," says Lathom, bemused. "Writers don't major in anything—they minor in everything, usually outside a classroom far away from so-called *teachers*. I've been to Blythe," he adds. "It's a shithole."

"So very glad you noticed." Blythe pauses.

"So, how do I become a writer?"

"I already told you. Write. A lot. Every day. And read. A lot. Every day. But only read *good* writing. And especially read the kind of books you'd like to write. Then write them instead of thinking about writing them. You can only learn to write autodidactically."

"Huh?"

"By teaching yourself. Sure, you can take English Lit, but the class will only be as good as the books they assign. In your case, I suggest you start with a vocabulary book."

Blythe waits for more, to no avail.

"There must be more to it."

"There is. But I'm not your friggin' English Lit professor," says Lathom, pausing briefly before adding, "Okay, only because we have too much time on our hands, I'll give you this."

Blythe steadies himself with youthful enthusiasm, hands gripped on the wheel, looking straight ahead.

"Find your voice."

Lathom says nothing more.

"That's it?"

"It," says Lathom. "Seems easy. But it's not. If you're writing in first person, who's telling the story? Your story-telling voice is crucial to success. If you're writing in third person, what's your style, your narrator's voice? It takes writers a long time to discover their writing voice, or, if they're writing in character, their protagonist's voice, whether it's omniscient or selective." He pauses. "It's the same as when an actor walks into an auditioning room. Those doing the auditioning know *immediately* whether that person is right for the part simply by their *look* and *body language*—an actor's version of *voice*. The script reading that follows is obligatory, an unavoidable waste of time. No voice, no engagement from your reader."

"But who's my reader?"

"Exactly. Notice I didn't say *readership*. I said *reader*."

"Why?"

"Because you can't please everyone. There's no point trying. Reading, like viewing art, is subjective. What one person loves, another hates. And that's another thing. You want your reader to either *love* or *hate* what you've written. Anything in between is a bore—and you *never* want to be boring."

"But who's my reader?"

"Please yourself. Don't pander. You're going to spend a

long time writing a novel—in my case, a *very* long time."
Lathom chuckles sourly. "You might as well amuse yourself, enjoy what you're writing about. Beyond that, choose
a person who you love and respect and who seems to like
you or whatever you write. This person should share your
sense of humor, your sense of irony. *That's* your reader. Write
specifically for that person, and no one else. And don't show
it to that person until it's done."

"Who do *you* write for?"

Lathom shifts with discomfort, a hint of a smirk on his
face, disguising a hurt. "A gal I knew a long, long time ago."

Blythe's phone sounds and he answers stiffly after recognizing the caller's identity.

"Yes, ma'am. Uh-huh. Everything's fine. We're on our
way." He pauses to listen to the voice on the other end. "Oh.
Okay. See you there." He disconnects and looks sideways at
Lathom. "That's interesting."

"What is?"

"My boss, Mulberry's head of publicity? She's in San
Francisco at a sales conference. She says she's coming to
your signing tonight."

Lathom smirks. *Finally, some adult supervision—and
attention from the higher-ups.*

"I think she wants to confirm you're really there," Blythe
adds. "So, I guess it's a good thing you decided to go."

Lathom bristles. "I had *other* reasons for making this trip."

"I know, I was there."

"You only know half of it."

"You want to tell me the other half?"

"No."

"In that case, can we talk some more about writing?"

"I lost my train of thought."

"You were talking about my readers."

"No. Your *one* reader. Period. Unless you hit the jackpot."

"What's that?"

"F. Scott knew—it's what we all strive for."

"Knew what?"

"That you're writing for the youth of your lifetime, librarians of the next generation, and professors every generation after that. And don't talk about what you're writing to *anyone*. Especially don't talk about it before you've started writing because it'll be all talk and you'll be sick of your story before you even start writing it. When you feel like talking, write instead—and write how you'd talk it, that may well be your voice. You got that? Write like you're standing at a bar telling a story to someone. And then let it rip. Pay no attention to grammar or punctuation or syntax or any other rules of writing. Just get the story out of your head and into words on paper. There's plenty of time later to stylize and revise. That'll be the second most important thing, after voice. Revision."

"Is there a *third* most important thing?"

"There's a *hundred* most important things. But the third most important is always choose the right word. And four, pay attention to rhythm, to crafting a good sentence in harmony with all the sentences around it. All those hundred things need to be a finely-tuned orchestra playing in sync with one another."

"Do you sketch your whole story in advance or do you make it up as you go along?"

"Yes."

Blythe chuckles.

"A story has to have structure," says Lathom. "And story is separate from writing. The best writing in the world will not necessarily tell a story. And the best story needs good writing to bring it alive. Call them twins. Without both, there's no novel. But it wouldn't be enjoyable for me to write if I always knew what was going to happen next." Lathom sighs.

"Writing—for me, anyway—is my own personal soap opera. This is not teamwork, God forbid. I'm the producer, the director and there's a part of me in every character because all of them derive from some part of my psyche, mixed with elements of other people I've known. When it's going good, it's like a movie playing in my head and I don't know what's going to happen next until I write it. That's what keeps it exciting and suspenseful for me. But without story structure, your reader will never engage. Your reader won't even know *why* he won't engage. It's a visceral thing that goes all the way back to Greek mythology."

"But isn't that writing to formula?"

"No." Lathom shakes his head with vehemence. "It's knowing the rules and being creative with them. Picasso taught us that you're allowed to break the rules only after you know them. And, God knows, there are a lot of writers who don't."

He glares straight ahead at the road. "Enough for now." Then he leans back, trying to find peace of mind, so often elusive, but all he can think about is that damn lawsuit and how much money he's going to waste defending himself.

15.

"KING City," Blythe announces. "The halfway mark—at least for San Francisco. I think I'll fill the tank."

Huddled around a Chevron station: McDonald's, Taco Bell, KFC and a few lesser-known fast-food shacks.

"Want something to eat?" asks Blythe, pumping gas.

"You must be kidding," says Lathom, aghast. "Is this what roadside America has come to? And no Starbucks?"

"Soledad," says Blythe.

"Huh?"

"Further on up the road. There's a Subway, too, if that works better for you."

"It doesn't. But I'd like some coffee."

And indeed, a short distance later, Soledad rolls up, and a Starbucks with it.

Inside, while ordering black coffee, out the corner of his eye Lathom recognizes someone he knows, compelling him to shrink into camouflage mode, at which he is proficient (in his mind, anyway), until coffee is poured and he can scurry back to the car, hopefully unnoticed.

***

"You look spooked," says Blythe, as he rejoins I-101. "What happened?"

"No, nothing," says Lathom.

"But you've turned pale, like you saw a ghost."

Lathom pulls a hankie from his pocket and wipes at his forehead. "Worse. I think I saw my daughter."

"Your daughter?"

"Don't want to talk about it." Lathom zips his lips closed with a forefinger.

They roll on in silence, until just under a half-hour later exit signs appear for Salinas.

"John Steinbeck's hometown," says Lathom. "His museum is here. Can we see it?"

Blythe checks the time. "We'd be cutting it close."

"I just want to see the truck he supposedly camped out in around the country with his dog, Charley."

"Supposedly?"

"I knew his son, Thom. He was a drinking buddy of mine in Montecito before Agent Orange from Vietnam finally caught up with him. And Thom told me his father would never have roughed it in a camper, maybe occasionally, but mostly stayed overnight in luxury hotels."

Blythe ramps off onto North Main Street and follows

it all the way through town until, at its end, the mostly glass-fronted National Steinbeck Center looms large.

Lathom nods. "Impressive. There are several Hemingway museums scattered around the country, but nothing like this. Literary politics," he adds, almost inaudibly.

Blythe parks and they alight, pay admission. Lathom beelines for the *Travels with Charley* exhibits, stopping at a large map that displays Steinbeck's 10,000-mile trek around the continental USA "in search of America."

And then those iconic wheels: a hunter-green pickup truck with a camper customized to Steinbeck's specs; an interior of mahogany with removable diner-style table for unfolding a couchette into a bed.

"You ever read it?" Lathom asks Blythe, peering into the camper.

Blythe shakes his head.

"You should. Quite likely the best road book ever written."

A quote from *Travels with Charley* prominently adorns a wall beside the truck: *We find after years of struggle that we do not take a trip; a trip takes us.*

"Ain't that the truth," Lathom mutters.

"Seen enough?" asks Blythe, checking the time on his phone.

"Jeez, you're like the Alice in Wonderland rabbit, only difference is you use a cell phone instead of a pocket watch. Yeah, okay, I've seen enough. Steinbeck saw enough, too. He knew the country was going to hell in a handbasket." Latham shakes his head. "I think every generation laments society's progress beyond the period in which they lived."

16.

Back on the road, Blythe tries to make up for lost time, tearing up 101, around San Jose.

"Here's another writing tip for you," says Lathom. "Thom Steinbeck once told me that his father used to make himself invisible in bars to eavesdrop on all the conversations going on around him."

"For story ideas?"

"Nada. For dialogue. You've got to cultivate an ear for how real people talk—and that's how Steinbeck did it. Each character in every story you write has his own way of talking. Some characters are succinct, others blabber on and on—and many varieties in between."

Interstate traffic slows as it winds into downtown San Francisco, consuming them amid rush-hour traffic, motorists striving to funnel onto the Golden Gate Bridge for passage into Marin County.

"I still don't understand why Mulberry Press didn't organize an event in Fog City," says Lathom, gesturing widely at the city streets. "This is near to where I lived when my last novel came out. The publisher threw a huge party for me at City Lights Bookstore and afterwards everyone got tanked at Vesuvio, where Kerouac and the Beats used to drink. Lawrence Ferlinghetti, the owner was right there with us." He looks at Blythe. "You've heard of them, I hope."

Blythe nods.

"Those were the days." Lathom recognizes a familiar intersection. "What say we make a quick stop at the Tadich Grill for a bowl of the world's best cioppino?"

"What's that?"

"Seafood stew. Invented by the Italian fishermen who settled Sausalito, more tomato-based than French bouillabaisse and twice as tasty."

Blythe checks the digital clock on his dashboard. "If I don't get you to Healdsburg on time, I'm toast. Especially with my boss coming in for this." He gestures at the gridlock before them. "Everyone's trying to get across the same bridge."

"Maybe stop in Sausalito then, first exit after the damn bridge?"

"The Golden Gate is only part of the problem." Blythe shakes his head in frustration. "This time of day, it'll be bumper-to-bumper until we get past Petaluma. Can't risk it."

"I once lived on a houseboat in Sausalito," says Lathom with whimsy. "Happiest time in my life."

Blythe perks to this. "Why?"

"That's where I wrote my first novel. And I wrote it on a houseboat I lived on with a gal I truly loved. That was long before I got hitched to a gal I grew to truly *not* love. And, ironically, it was the success of my novel that broke us up."

"Really?"

"Truly. Literary success went to my head and fame turned me into an asshole for a while. Hanging out with Peter Fonda, for chrissakes. Staying out all night drinking, playing around. I was so high on myself, I walked around like I owned the mission." He pauses. "I often think about what happened to her."

"Your ex-wife?"

"Hell no," snaps Lathom. "Not that bitch. My Sausalito sweetheart. She brewed the best tasting coffee I've ever had. It's true. She would grind freshly roasted beans by hand in a wooden mill." He shakes his head, smiling in appreciation. "And she also flipped the world's finest blueberry pancakes, and always with the most amazing…" he pauses… "the most amazing smile." Lathom smiles himself, a rare occurrence, at the thought. "Remember I said that every writer needs a sole reader to write for?"

"I do."

"That gal was mine—my reader. Still is. Even for my new novel."

This bewilders Blythe. "You're still in contact with her?"

"Sadly, no."

"So why don't you try to find her?"

"How?"

"Facebook, maybe?"

Lathom cringes. "I don't do Facebook."

"Why not?"

"It's a hypnotic trap, created for people who can't cultivate a genuine audience. Most of the people on it aren't your real friends, and those who are, well, they won't be for long. You begin to loath them and they loath you after everyone discovers their real beliefs about politics and religion and how obnoxious they can be about expressing those beliefs and their boasts about vacations, new cars and life in general. People aren't nearly as brutal or as show-offish in person."

"But if you're not on Facebook," says Blythe. "How do you know all this?"

"From one of the coffee Neanderthals who used to work there, now retired in Montecito. He told me he wouldn't allow his own kids to use it. What does that tell you?"

"So why not try to find her by other means?"

Lathom shrugs. "I did, a long time ago, after my marriage failed and I realized how special she was." He shakes his head. "Took me long enough. Too long, I guess, because there was no trace of her. I eventually gave up." He pauses. "What's the story on her, anyway?"

"On who?"

"Your boss, the publicity honcho at Mulberry."

"Oh. Francine Fassbender. She's tough. Word is, the

last publicity chief—her old boss—hired and mentored her, and then Francine stabbed him in the back, got him fired, supposedly for making sexual advances toward her. That's the office gossip, anyway."

Lathom sighs. "The history of the world."

Blythe hits the brakes hard as another driver turning from a side-street cuts him off. "Sonofabitch!" He honks his horn and the other driver flips him the bird. "Jeez, can you believe that guy?"

Lathom chuckles. "World's full of them."

Ten minutes later, the tall orange-vermillion arches loom up ahead and, before they know it, author and media escort are whizzing across the magnificent Golden Gate into Marin County.

"Only one man ever survived this jump," says Lathom. "And now he travels the country lecturing on why *not* to jump. Remember that with your writing. Life is irony. And vice versa."

"You ever consider jumping?" Blythe throws Lathom a sideways glance.

The author glares straight ahead. "Not until this book tour. Thanks for the suggestion."

The road curves, first moving swiftly, then congesting once again, stops and starts. And the exit to Sausalito goes ignored as Blythe fights the clock in fear of Francine Fassbender.

17.

Lathom steadies himself from the rigors of the road in the minimalist bare-bones bar of Hotel Healdsburg. With only a few minutes before the six o'clock event, he savors his alone time along with Anejo tequila, a few rocks and a slice of lime while contemplating the presumed humiliation-to-come.

And then, at the appointed hour, Blythe reappears.

"I've got a great room!" the media escort says with much enthusiasm. "Hardwood floors, teak plantation shutters—and the best bathroom plumbing I've ever seen. I wish I could stay here a whole week!"

Lathom sips from his glass, less enthusiastic about the digs if amused by his escort's enthusiasm.

"If only I could figure out how to use the TV remote," he mutters, draining the last of his tequila. "I can barely understand how the lighting works."

"Would you like me to show you?" offers Blythe.

Lathom growls a *nah* and waves away the offer. He rises, steadies his nerves and feels at his pants pocket. "Damn! Where's my Purell?"

Blythe shrugs. "Maybe you left it in the car?"

"Can you check?"

Blythe goes out to the forecourt where the Ford Escape is parked and returns empty-handed.

"Is there a pharmacy around here?" asks Lathom, his eyes desperate with fear.

"Probably," says Blythe, "but we don't have time to stop anywhere. It's already past six. We've really got to go."

Resigned to the germs that may soon invade and plague him, Lathom walks unhappily with Blythe through the town Plaza—an old-time square with a gazebo and a flagpole, stars and stripes fluttering—across the road to Copperfield's.

It is dark—being mid-November—and the glow of the bookstore's display window is resplendent with a few dozen copies of *Day of the Rabbits*. The books are interspersed with an assortment of both stuffed and porcelain bunnies, a decorative touch of Easter in mid-autumn that leaves Lathom discombobulated.

"The sons-of-bitches haven't read it," he fumes in dismay, turning in disgust from the window. "My novel has nothing to do with rabbits, for chrissakes!"

Blythe clucks quietly. Like a rabbit.

Lathom turns to his escort, studying him. "What the hell are you doing?"

"You already know," Blythe sniffles. "It's involuntary—my aboiment thing."

"But these aren't even real rabbits!"

"We talked about that in the car, remember?" Blythe shrugs. "Sometimes just an image of an animal sparks a reaction in my brain."

"Whatever." Lathom seethes, his gaze refocused on the window display. "Aside from being juvenile, this ridiculous exhibit is false advertising!"

Blythe cringes when he peers through the door and sees his boss, Francine Fassbender, who looks like a character only Lily Tomlin might have concocted based on Cruella de Vil, tall and stern-faced beneath a short, mannish hairstyle and a sneer of a smile.

Dutifully, Blythe walks straight up to her, with Lathom alongside, and introduces the Mulberry author.

Madam Fassbender looks Lathom up and down, as if assessing his suitability to appear in public, with an expression that suggests disdain.

Mulberry's author is wearing his trademark black shirt and trousers, safari vest and straw fedora—none of it, clearly, to Francine's liking.

She sniffs—*and is that body odor?*

"You're late," she snaps at Lathom before turning on Blythe with a sneer. "My instructions were very clear: arrive twenty minutes early to sign a stack of books for this bookstore."

"I'm sorry, I…"

"Never mind," she snaps. "I have no patience for excuses." She reverts her contemptuous gaze upon the author. "Only solutions. And here's the solution: you'll have to stay behind and do it afterwards."

Lathom is appalled by the schoolmarmish manner with which he is addressed.

Detention?

"We'll see about that," he says under his breath, resisting a temptation to walk out, here and now. *Nice to meet you too—bitch-witch.*

Francine has short auburn hair—very short—with an enduring scowl, snake eyes that appear to be looking for someone to bite, and a body language taut with venom needing release.

"Shall we get started?" says the female bookshop manager who had been conversing with Francine.

Some dozen-plus persons are scattered throughout the thirty wooden chairs assembled in tidy rows.

Lathom takes the lectern and grimly studies those gathered before him.

"Just so you know," he says, scowling, after a long thirty seconds, "my novel has nothing to do with rabbits."

This elicits a chuckle or two from the audience.

"And there's nothing funny about it, either," he continues, acerbically. "My novel is not a comedy. The title, with the word *rabbits*, is a metaphor—for what, you'll find out if you read the book." He points at the window behind them and pauses. "So please don't be misled by cute bunnies in the window."

A hand raises. "What *is* the book about?" asks a middle-aged female.

"The book—my writing—speaks for itself," replies Lathom. "Which means, if you want to know what it's about, you actually have to *read* it. As my old friend, the master of the novella Jim Harrison used to say, 'Nothing matters but the work itself.' Or put another way, by Bruce Springsteen, 'Look at the art, not the artist.'"

"Then why are you here?" asks an elderly male, causing a new round of guffaws.

"I wish I knew," says Lathom, shrugging his shoulders. He points to Francine Fassbender, standing at the back with Blythe and the shop manager flanking her on either side. "Ask *her.*"

Francine's grimace deepens; not amused, she, a brief blush followed by a contemptuous laugh. And then, composing herself, she says, "Perhaps you'd like to do a reading from your novel, Mister Lathom?"

Lathom glares at her, eyeballs connecting, locking, not letting go.

"Perhaps not, madam. Do I look like a capuchin monkey dancing to the tune of an organ grinder?"

All necks swerve to Francine as the audience eagerly follows this tennis match of barbs.

"I think these folks," continues Lathom, "are perfectly capable of reading books for themselves. Or they wouldn't be here, in a bookstore."

Francine finally breaks the eye-lock, trembling with anger.

Some of the audience continue to chuckle nervously, though a corpulent man who'd been dragged along by his wife lets rip a big belly laugh, having not expected to be so thoroughly entertained.

"I'll answer a few more questions, if you have any," Lathom adds. "And I'll sign your books if you really believe my signature adds some worth to what I've written. And then I hope to be able to get back to doing what writers are supposed to do. Write. Not pose and blabber."

"Who's your favorite author?" asks another member of the audience.

"That's too shallow to deserve a response," replies Lathom. "Would you also like to know my favorite color?"

"I'm sorry, Mister Lathom, I'll re-phrase my question. Which writers have most influenced your writing?"

"I'm not easily influenced," says Lathom, shifting his weight. "Especially not by other authors. Such a question implies my ideas are not self-generated or original. Norman Mailer, some of whose novels I respect, was famous for saying that he never reads anything while writing a novel. You know why? Because he didn't want to be influenced by another writer's style or ideas. And Mailer was *always* writing a novel."

"What do you make of Kirkus panning your novel?" asks another.

"I don't pay attention to whatever anyone writes about my works," replies Lathom. "As Jim Harrison used to say, 'The goose trying to lay golden eggs shouldn't be using a mirror to look at its butt.'"

"If your book is not about rabbits, is it possibly about cats?" asks the belly-laugher, in search, no doubt, of another comical moment.

Lathom does not reply. Quite the opposite, he tightly purses his lips. For if there is one main thing Lathom's ego cannot abide, it is being mocked.

A long ten seconds pass.

"Again, I quote Jim Harrison," he finally says. "Everywhere we are witness to the extreme confidence some people have in their stupidities." He pauses briefly. "I hope you read my book and discover for yourself whether this novel is about rabbits or cats."

And with that, the author brusquely stalks around his gathered guests, glowers momentarily at Francine Fassbender and exits out the door, leaving a miasma in his wake.

18.

INSIDE Hotel Healdsburg's bar, Lathom grabs a stool and resumes drinking Anejo tequila. As he nurses the amber-colored libation, Blythe bounds in with two armfuls of books and a blue Sharpie marker.

"Francine says to sign these," he says.

"*Ya vol!*" Lathom salutes like a Nazi.

After signing the eleventh copy he looks up. "But there weren't this many people there."

"You're right, there weren't." Blythe nods. "My boss wants a bunch more signed for the *shelves*."

Lathom one-eyes his escort. "Why?"

"She says unsold signed books can't be returned from the bookstore to the publisher for a refund, so you should sign as many as possible."

Lathom harrumphs, offended by the notion of a bookstore having to return an unsold copy of his book.

In the midst of his signing copies, a whoosh of negative energy sweeps into the bar.

Francine Fassbender, pale as a ghost, confronts the author, oblivious of creating a spectacle in front of the bartender and other assorted patrons at the bar.

"You are... you are..." she sputters.

"Obstreperous?" says Lathom. "Indeed, I am."

"And what would you call your *appearance* this evening?" she barks.

Lathom regards her with an uncharacteristic blaseness. "Ephemeral?"

"I'd call it a breach of contract!"

"Nice try but no chance. I showed up."

"Yes!" shrills Francine. "You showed up and embarrassed me in front of an important bookseller! Do you have any idea how many Copperfields there are?"

"To my mind, only one," says Lathom, keeping his cool. "And that would be *David* Copperfield. Heard of *him?*"

"Well, I'm sorry to inform you, Mister Lathom, but Copperfield's is the largest independent bookselling chain on the West Coast, which is why I'm here this evening, in-person."

"Who cares?" Lathom shrugs. "I have my own theory about why you're here, *in person.*"

Francine puts both hands on her hips. "And that would be?"

"To check up on me."

Francine laughs sourly. "Don't compliment yourself,

mister. I have no interest in *authors*." She contorts her mouth to over-enunciate the word *authors*. "My interest is retaining good relations with *booksellers*."

"Excuse me?" says Lathom, somewhat astounded by her position.

"You heard right."

"You're saying that Mulberry Press cares more about the people who sell their books than the authors who write them?"

"In your case, especially," taunts Francine, bristling. "Welcome to the twenty-first century, Mister Lathom. Glad you deigned to come out of mothballs and rediscover contemporary book publishing. We're all terribly sorry it's not to your liking, but there you go."

"There *I* go? Might *you* cease bombinating me with your blatherskite, woman, and *you* just go?"

Francine re-grabs her hips. "Are you for real?"

"Am *I* for real? I bet putting rabbits in the bookstore window was *your* very *unreal* idea. And you're asking if *I'm* for real?"

Francine dismisses him with a backhand. "I don't know what on earth you're talking about."

"More sibilation," says Lathom before a new thought hits him. "Have you even *read* my novel?"

"I'm not going to dignify that with an answer."

"Ha! I should have known. Of course, you haven't."

"And have *you* happened to see today's LA Times?" demands Francine, introducing a tone of faux sweetness into her rant.

Lathom shrugs with nonchalance. "I've been on the road all day after surviving a mudslide. You'll forgive me if I'm a wee be out of touch."

"I have no doubt you're out of touch," Francine says with a fake laugh. "But you may want to get back in touch with reality and read the LA Times review of your novel, not least because its contents will most certainly be a part of my report to Mulberry's president, publisher and director of sales."

"You're reporting me?" Lathom asks in mock horror. "Ha! First detention, now I'm being reported!"

"My report will also include an account of this evening's debacle."

And with that parting shot, Francine storms off, almost tripping on one of her high-heels.

Lathom cups his hand and calls after her. "May all your demons come true!" Then he turns to Blythe. "She can suck my corkscrew. And what's this about a review in the LA Times?"

"Looks like we sold nine books tonight," says Blythe, pretending he hadn't heard the question as he hastily departs with a stack of signed books.

Lathom rises to search for a copy of the *Los Angeles Times* but all the hotel can muster is *USA Today*.

So, somewhat impatiently, he sips Anejo awaiting Blythe's return.

19.

"THE LA Times," Lathom says, tapping his hand when his media escort reappears. "Can you access it on your phone?"

"I can," he says sheepishly. "But I'd rather not."

"And why is that?"

"Because, to be honest, Mister Lathom, I don't think you're going to like what the LA Times wrote about you and your new novel. And I don't want what they published to interfere with the rest of your book tour."

"You've seen it?"

Blythe nods solemnly. "Uh-huh."

"I'm a grown man, sonny—out with it."

Blythe gulps. "There's a photo of you with your back to a bunch of empty chairs with a caption."

"What caption?"

"*Christopher Lathom makes an un-comeback.*"

Lathom grimaces.

"An *un-comeback?* What kind of English is that?"

Blythe shrugs.

"What next?" asks Lathom.

"It directs the reader to a review inside."

"Okay, okay—what's inside?"

"You won't like that either." Blythe pauses.

"Tell me."

"The review is titled *No Rabbits Here.*"

"Enough," snaps Lathom.

"Bartender!" he calls out. "Another tequila. Now!"

He turns to Blythe.

"That's why it's good to be in the booze business. People drink to celebrate, people drink to commiserate. Good times or bad, the answer is booze. To hell with the goddam LA Times."

"We've got a long haul tomorrow," says Blythe, gently, cautiously. "Gotta start early."

"Really, now," says a wild-eyed Lathom. "And where, may I ask, is this hayride to doom supposed to take us next?"

"Ashland, Oregon."

"Ashland, Oregon. But of course. How could I be so stupid to even ask." He pauses. "They could have sent me to Chicago or Houston, Miami or Boston—and they're sending me to... where? Ass-land, Oregon? No wonder this tour is a crock full of nuts. Is it Mulberry—or that horrible woman—what's her name?"

"Francine."

"Is Francine purposely trying to sabotage me?"

Blythe smirks. "If she wasn't before, she'll certainly try after this evening."

"Doesn't matter," snaps Lathom. "I'm not sure things could get much worse."

"Umm, they already have."

"Have what?"

"Gotten worse."

Lathom shakes his head. "Another bad review?"

"No."

"Then what?"

"We have to take my boss's niece with us to Portland."

"What?"

"Sorry, Francine just told me a couple minutes ago."

"Why?"

"She was supposed to take her niece to Portland her-self—family time, Francine isn't married…"

"Why am I not surprised?"

"… but Francine was called back to New York for urgent business, or so she says, so she asked me to drive her niece."

"You? What about asking *my* permission?"

Blythe shrugs.

"Well, I hope you and…"

"Her name is Jasmine."

"I wish you and Jasmine bon voyage."

"What does that mean?"

"It means finito bon soir. I'm outta this nuthouse-on-wheels."

"I don't think you want to do that." says Blythe.

"Be careful what you think."

"I mean, seriously, you'd be playing right into my boss's hands. She's looking for a reason to freeze your advance."

Lathom's eyeballs pop, appalled. "You know about *that*?"

"I overheard my boss talking to *her* boss after you walked out on your audience this evening. I get the feeling she'd love nothing better."

"I did *not* walk out on my audience." Now Lathom is perplexed.

"Well, you left early and abruptly without saying goodbye while everyone was still sitting."

Lathom vehemently shakes his head.

"What would you call it?" Blythe adds.

"What would I call it? I'd call it an enervation."

"A what?"

"An energy-suck," Lathom snorts. "The audience was responsible for terminating my appearance with their inane line of questioning, instigated by bunny rabbits in the window, which was even more inane. Under the circumstances, I was well within my rights to beat a hasty departure."

20.

LATHOM is awakened by the ringing of his room phone on a bedside table.

He answers just to stop it pounding on his head. "What?"

"Where are you?" asks Blythe.

"In my room, obviously."

"Well, we're ready to roll and we've got at least a six-hour drive ahead of us—remember?"

"Okay, okay." Lathom replaces the receiver, his head aching worse than before, especially when he rolls unsteadily out of bed. He splashes his face with cold water, skips a shower, fumbles with yesterday's clothes and descends to the lobby, disheveled and bleary-eyed.

Blythe and Jasmine, Francine Fassbender's niece, await him in the lobby.

Jasmine is about twenty-eight, fresh faced with a caramel-rose complexion, with long light brown hair mostly braided into a pony-tail, except on the sides where it hangs freely over her ears. Her eyes are bright and clear and her smile is as naturally blithesome as it is endearing, with straight white teeth, evoking Iowa cornfields.

And she is delicately perfumed with a fragrant aroma— maybe tuberose?

"Mister Lathom?" She thrusts out her hand. "A pleasure to meet you, sir."

With some trepidation, he limply shakes her soft hand, wondering where he put his Purell, then recalling that it got misplaced.

"Let's hit the road," says Blythe impatiently.

"What's the hurry?" says Jasmine sweetly. "It's about the journey, not the destination, no?"

Lathom rolls his eyes. "Trust me, young lady, this journey sucks dead donkey dicks and you can quote me on that. No," he catches, himself, "you're *not allowed* to quote me. On anything. Everything I say is confidential—got that?"

"No," says Blythe, shaking his head in embarrassment. "This journey *is* about the destination." He dutifully plucks Lathom's travel bag from the floor and places it in the trunk where his and Jasmine's things have already been stowed.

"I've got to get my author to his gig on time," he adds. "My job depends on it."

"I'm so excited," says Jasmine, climbing into the back seat.

"About his gig?"

"No, about driving past Mount Shasta—it's on the way.

I've been wanting to feel the mystical energy of Shasta for a long time. Did you know it's a real volcano?"

"As opposed to a fake one?" asks Lathom sardonically.

Jasmine turns and comes face-to-face with Scallywag, albeit separated by glass. "Wow! What's this?"

Lathom turns from the front seat. "My bearded dragon is a who, not a what. First a mudslide, now a volcanic mountain. With my luck, it'll probably blow while we're there. What's so damn mystical about it?"

"Well, for a start, Mount Shasta is located on one of planet Earth's main chakras."

"Oh, dear," says Lathom. "I had a feeling we might be going in that direction."

"Because of that, it has magical energy," adds a wide-eyed Jasmine. "May I hold him?"

"Scallywag? Wait till he gets used to your presence. But do me a favor and drop this into his aquarium, he's probably hungry." Lathom passes a wad of lettuce scrounged from the hotel kitchen. "He bites spies. So be careful."

"What's that supposed to mean?" asks Jasmine.

"Oh, you want to play Miss Innocent?"

"Spy on who?" she asks.

"Me."

"Me-me-me!" Jasmine laughs winsomely. "Sorry if it hurts your ego, Mister Lathom, but in a word, *no*, I'm not here to spy on you, or anyone else. Why on earth would I want to do that?"

"Because your Aunt Francine is trying to fuck me."

Jasmine studies Lathom for several seconds. "Given your age and looks, you should be complimented by that," says Jasmine, leaving Lathom in awe of this whipper-snapper's quick wit, rendering him somewhat speechless.

"Ouch," says Blythe, grinning, eyes focused on plotting the trip through his phone map, pinpointing the best horizontal routes across a state whose arteries are mostly vertical.

Finally, he ignites the car, pulls out and stops briefly at a red light before turning north onto Healdsburg Avenue.

"What do you do, Jasmine?" asks Blythe.

"I'm studying to be a yoga teacher."

"Cool."

"Yoga." Lathom scoffs. "You and everybody else of your generation. Isn't yoga just an excuse to *do nothing?*"

Jasmine ignores the question. "What I'd really like to do is live in a monastery for a few months, maybe longer. That's why I'm excited about this trip. There's a Buddhist monastery near Mount Shasta I want to scout out, see if they'll let me stay overnight sometime."

"Taking over this road trip, are you, missy?" says Lathom. "Like aunt, like niece."

"No detour necessary," says Jasmine. "It's on the way. I'd like to see if the solitude of a monastery is truly the best way for people to get in tune with themselves."

"By turning your back on the world?" It immediately dawns on Lathom that a solitary existence as a writer has been his own path. The irony

Jasmine shakes her head. "It's not about escaping reality."

"Then what?"

"It's about giving yourself the time and space to *better understand* reality. It's about awakening your inner senses then *re-joining* reality with a better overall sense of yourself. It's about yielding to something much greater—a personal experience with God."

"Whose god?" asks Lathom, amused.

"There's only one God," says Jasmine.

"Of course," Lathom chuckles. "Yours."

"Mine, yours and everyone else's," says Jasmine. "It's the same God for all of us, whether who knows it or not, deriving from one source, with different interpretations. I've studied these things."

"In your studies, young lady, have you per chance encountered Friedrich Nietzsche?"

"I don't think so."

"Nietzsche was a German philosopher, famous for saying *God is dead.*"

"I don't think that's true."

"And what Nietzsche meant was, the *belief* in God, by rational people, was dead, due to advances in material science during the renaissance. Meaning, there *never was* a God."

"Nietzsche was wrong."

Lathom laughs. "*All* his philosophical treatises?"

"I don't know about all of them. But he was definitely wrong about God never existing."

"Oh dear, are you one of those *Born Agains*?"

"No."

"Or maybe a strict Catholic upbringing?"

Jasmine shakes her head. "No, sorry. I only said I'd like to stay in a monastery for a while. My parents were Methodists, but they didn't push their beliefs on me. I'm not religious, I'm spiritual."

"What's the difference?"

"Hierarchy." She pauses. "I don't believe anyone needs a middleman to connect with God. Or churches or temples or mosques. We are already in God's house, just *being*."

"But monasteries are okay?"

"All places of worship are okay, full of positive energy from prayer. I'm just saying you don't need them to connect to God."

"Can you describe God?" Lathom asks.

"Of course," Jasmine replies. "Just look out the window."

"Up to heaven?"

"No, silly—everywhere."

"Ah, so you're a pantheist."

Now Jasmine laughs. "You're trying to pin a label on me. Truth is, I'm a free spirit without a slot."

"Do you get all this from yoga?"

"No, but yoga bolsters the Eastern traditions and beliefs, which go hand in hand not only with spirituality and godliness but also with the beliefs of the mystical factions of the great Western religions. Yoga provides a more mindful link between body and soul."

"So," says Lathom, "You're a New Ager."

Jasmine chuckles.

"Just another label. How about if I label you *grumpy old author?*"

Blythe laughs.

Lathom throws his driver an irritated glance, then circles back to Jasmine. "So, what awaits you in Portland?"

"I want to see Povey Brothers stained glass."

"Who?"

"The Povey Brothers. They're renowned as the Tiffany of the Northwest and some of their finest stained glass is still in Portland, where they had their studio. But I'm even more excited about visiting Ashlantis."

"Where?"

"Ashland," Blythe pipes up. "Tonight's destination. Some people think of it as a spiritual resurrection of the mystical island of Atlantis, hence the nickname."

Lathom faces Blythe. "Ah, Ass-land, the chosen venue for my book event." He turns to Jasmine in the backseat. "Your aunt is nuts."

"Aunt Francine is very nice to me," counters Jasmine.

Lathom is about to respond but, interrupted by his chiming phone, chooses his literary agent, Downey, for interaction instead. He answers as Blythe swings onto Highway 128.

"What did you *do* last night?" Downey pre-empts the usual authorial pre-empt.

"What did *I* do?" says Lathom. "I don't know where to begin. But maybe I should start with bunny rabbits in the display window."

"Mulberry Press is claiming you've breached your contract."

"What? How so?"

"They say you walked out on your audience. They want to disown you!"

"Story of my life." Lathom sighs. "Does that mean I can turn around and go home?"

"No, don't do that! As long as you show up they know they can't legally hold up your advance, even if you leave early. But can't you try to be a little more accommodating?"

"Accommodating? How about *they* try to accommodate *me*? Their own publicity chief hasn't even bothered to read my novel, for chrissakes!"

"And I don't think she ever will from the sound of things," says Downey. "My main focus right now is the advance. Stick with the book tour, show up where you're scheduled to appear and let's get paid. Where are you now?"

"On the way to a place called Ass-lantis."

"*Where?*"

"Exactly. Only God knows why they've booked me there." He glances at Jasmine, already regretting his choice of words. "Goodbye." Lathom disconnects. "And good riddance," he mutters.

"Interesting." Jasmine pipes up from the backseat.

"Which part?"

"Your invocation of God."

"I should have known you'd make it an issue." Lathom waves her away. "Just a figure of speech."

"Maybe you should just surrender to the universe," says Jasmine.

"Trust me, young lady," says Lathom, shaking his head in exasperation. "I gave up a long time ago."

"Then surrender to the moment."

"Which moment?"

"This moment."

"That moment, a moment ago? It's already gone."

"You know what I mean."

"I'm glad I don't."

"Surrender to this trip. You're exactly where you're supposed to be."

"On my way to Ass-lantis?"

"In this car, right now, with us—a road trip."

"You're saying I'm supposed to be *happy* about being here?" says Lathom.

"Where else would you be happier?" Jasmine gestures out the window at rolling green hills covered with rows and rows of grape vines. "It's gorgeous out here in Napa!"

Lathom considers the answer: My village, the circuit, Starbucks, Von's, even Neanderthal's Coffee, *sans* mud...

Says he, "Why should I be happy being forced to take a book tour by a publisher that has done such a shitty job putting it together? They have deracinated me!"

"Huh?" says Jasmine.

"Deracinate!"

"Huh?" says Blythe

"Look it up!" snaps Lathom.

"Don't over-excite yourself," says Jasmine. "Why don't you just take a few deep breaths and enjoy the ride?"

"Don't try to suck me into your do-nothing yoga nonsense."

"Breathing is fundamental to everyone, not just to those who practice yoga," says Jasmine. "Think about it. You can go for weeks without eating food. You can go for days without drinking water. But you can go only a few minutes without breathing air. Oxygen is the most precious thing we have. Why not fill your lungs with it, pay attention to the process of breathing and clear your head of all the negative bullshit it seems to be full of?"

Blythe bursts out laughing, not so much from Jasmine's harsh words, but by the sweetness with which she delivered them.

"C'mon," continues Jasmine. "Let's all breathe. Take a deep breath through your nose."

Blythe complies.

Lathom does not.

"Lungs full?" Jasmine coaches. "Now exhale. Slowly. Come on, you too, Mister Lathom."

"You may call me Chris." Reluctantly, Lathom joins in and takes a deep breath, mildly captivated by this whipper-snapper.

"Through your nose," Jasmine coaches. "Out your mouth. Three times. May I be blunt with you, Chris?"

"Like you haven't been already?"

"Your breath is really bad, like, putrid."

Blythe exhales explosively with laughter.

Lathom blushes. "That's what I get for engaging in your antics? Insults?"

"I don't mean to insult you, Chris. I'm only trying to help."

"Help how?"

"Help cure your bad breath—especially if we're going to be together in this car all the way to Portland."

"This is my ride, honey, you're just a guest." Lathom pauses. "But, okay, let's say I neglected to brush my teeth this morning because *he...*" Lathom points at Blythe... "rushed me up and out—on a road trip I don't even want to be on."

"Just because you're not happy about taking this trip doesn't mean you should neglect your personal hygiene *and* make us suffer," says Jasmine. "First of all, I bet you sleep with your mouth *open.*"

Lathom shrugs. "Maybe, partly."

"Sleeping with your mouth open causes it to dry up and bad breath is the result of a dry mouth. Breathing through your mouth is also bad for your lungs."

"Oh, great—now my lungs are involved?"

"Of course." Jasmine nods earnestly. "Our mouths aren't equipped to process the air we breathe. Unlike our noses, our mouths cannot prepare the air for our lungs."

"No?"

"No. Your nose moistens and warms the air you breathe and, more important, the hair in your nose filters out germs."

Now she has Lathom's attention.

"Which is a good reason," she adds, "for keeping your mouth shut."

Blythe laughs. "Sounds better than Purell!"

"Wise-ass." Lathom swings his head between Jasmine and Blythe and back again to study his driver. "I'm glad you're both having a good time. At my expense, I might add, even though *you*," he gestures at Blythe, "only have this job because of *me*, and *you*, young lady, are getting a free ride because of *me*."

"There you go again," says Jasmine, "Me-me-me! What kind of mouthwash do you use—assuming you use any?"

Lathom rolls his eyes. "Of course I do."

"What brand?"

"Listerine."

"Uh-huh," says Jasmine. "That's part of the problem. Listerine has *alcohol* in it."

"That's a good thing," says Lathom. "Alcohol kills germs."

"Yes, alcohol kills germs. And it freshens your breath. Temporarily. But the alcohol dries your mouth—and dry mouth is what causes chronic bad breath like yours."

"You don't use mouthwash?"

"I use alcohol-*free* mouthwash. And I also recommend flouride-free toothpaste."

"For my breath?"

"No, for your pineal gland.'

"My what?"

"Pineal. P-i-n-e-a-l. It's a tiny gland at the base of your

brain about the size of a grain of rice. It is also the seat of your soul, where your consciousness resides."

Lathom harrumphs. "Assuming you know what you're talking about, young lady, what does that have to do with fluoride?"

"Simple. Fluoride calcifies the pineal gland, which in turn hardens your soul. I'll venture to guess you've been using fluoride toothpaste all your life."

Blythe laughs again and pounds his steering wheel, so mirthful, he.

A stony-faced Lathom studies his highly amused escort. "I hope you know where you're going."

In fact, Blythe neglected to take a left turn onto Highway 29 and as they're now rolling into the town of Calistoga, he realizes they are off-course. He pulls over to study his smart phone map, realizes his mistake and wordlessly executes a three-point turn to set the vehicle right.

"I thought not," says Lathom. He swings his head around to address Jasmine. "I suppose you're now going to tell me I can buy toothpaste *without* fluoride."

"Of course. Fluoride-free toothpaste. That's what I use."

"But isn't the water supply fluoridated?"

"Some is, some isn't," says Jasmine. "Depends on the state and county. Best thing is, get a water filter to filter out the fluoride—or drink bottled water. But be careful which brand because a lot of bottled water contains fluoride. Now, back to breathing."

"Must we?" says Lathom.

"We must, because we're coming to the most important part for eradicating putrid breath, which is breathing through your nose. If you've been breathing through your mouth for a long time, which I strongly suspect you've been doing, it means the receptors inside your nostrils have closed up, making it difficult for you to breathe through your nose. But if you push yourself to breathe the right way, through your nose, after a week or two the receptors in your nostrils will open up again. For now, just blow your nose a lot and use an inhaler until you get where you need to be."

"I need to be at my desk, writing," says Lathom. "Not driving in a car being lectured about how to breathe."

"But I thought you were giving it up," says Blythe.

"Writing? Nonsense. It's *publishing* I'm giving up."

"Hey look!" says Blythe, pointing to a sign on the corner of Foothill Drive and Berry Street. "A book drive!"

"That's poetic," says Jasmine. "A book drive while we're taking a book drive. We should check it out."

Lathom, mildly interested, does not protest.

Two blocks on, Blythe swings left into the grounds of Calistoga Elementary School and parks. The trio alight and wade into tables laden with stacks of books, uncategorized with barely any order. No one else is around save a couple of book drive volunteers.

"Look what I found!" Jasmine excitedly breaks their silence, holding a book high above her head.

"What is it?" asks Blythe.

"A novel by Chris Lathom—King Zero!"

"Let me see that," says Lathom, briskly walking over to Jasmine. He lifts the hardcover with its tattered jacket from her hands and flips through the first few pages.

"I don't believe it." He looks up at his fellow road warriors. "This is a *first edition*." His eyes revert to the book and he opens it, fixates on the price, which is penciled onto the top right-hand corner of the first page, and shakes his head in dismay. "For one dollar?"

"It's mine," says Jasmine, repossessing the book from Lathom's grip. "And you're going to sign it for me so it'll be worth *two* dollars!"

Lathom cringes, horrified by the low value placed upon his legacy.

While Jasmine pays for her prize, Blythe asks the money-taker what they'll do with the books they don't sell.

"It's a problem, honey," she replies in a voice scratchy from decades of nicotine. "The school library already took what they needed. First, we'll put them by the side of the road for anyone to go through, take what they want. But the rest…" she adds, shaking her head. "We'll have to pay someone to cart them all away to the dump."

Lathom, listening in, continues to shake his own head in horrified awe. "I've heard enough." He turns, even more disgusted than before and returns to the car ahead of his companions.

A few minutes later, rolling up the road, Lathom snaps out of his silent funk.

"Now I know how Wyatt Earp felt must have felt," he says.

"Wyatt Earp from the Old West?" asks Blythe.

"Was there another Wyatt Earp?"

"I guess not."

"People think he was a lawman," Lathom continues. "That's the legend and, like history, legends are lies agreed upon, to quote Napoleon. Truth is, Wyatt was a saloon keeper, and that was an important job because saloons, in those days, were important cultural and recreational centers. You know why?" He doesn't wait for a response. "Because saloons came with gambling and women. But by the time Wyatt hit eighty years old, in the late 1920s, gambling was illegal, prostitution was illegal in most states, and Prohibition had outlawed alcohol. Can you imagine how such social senescence must have made him feel?"

Lathom laughs. "He must have thought the Wild West—and the rest of the country—had gone to hell in a handbasket!"

"Senescence?" asks Blythe, scratching his head.

"It means deterioration," says Lathom. His phone begins to chime. "In other words, the opposite of so-called progress." He recognizes the number and answers.

"Glenn Pioche," says his intellectual property lawyer. "How are you today?"

"Unruly—unless you have good news. Please tell me you've resolved this nonsense."

"I can't because I haven't," replies Pioche. "They're not budging from the figure they mentioned to your lawyer in Santa Barbara. They seem to know you're doing a book tour and that you'll pay them what they want just to avoid any negative publicity."

"You see? They really are shakedown con artists. Is any of this public yet?"

"We have to assume they're trying. They'd probably settle for twenty-five thousand if they don't have to do any more work on the case."

"That's outrageous! For one tiny photo that someone else put on my Amazon page?"

"It's still up, they pointed out."

"Of course it is! I don't know how to take it down! Same as I don't know how to put one up!"

"I believe you," says Pioche. "It's a scam—the kind of thing that gives lawyers a bad name. Copyright law is archaic and the penalties are draconian. Intellectual property lawyers have become the new personal injury charlatans. Copyright ownership needs to be readdressed and reconfigured. These litigant photographers can't make an honest living by taking photographs anymore so they try to make a dishonest living by trolling the Internet, looking to see where their images have landed after putting them into the public domain themselves—and then they threaten or file lawsuits for a pay-off. The problem is, if they can prove a connection between you and that photo, a jury might find you guilty—and, with a copyright infringement, they're allowed to demand their legal fees be awarded against you."

"*Their* legal fees?"

"Yes."

"So, what's our next move?"

"After I submit a Response to their Claim?"

"Yes."

"Discovery. They'll demand a list of documents they believe will help them prove their case. It'll be extensive, to harass you as much as possible. And also, interrogatories. Written questions you have to answer under penalty of perjury—a kind of pre-testimony in advance of depositions."

"Sounds to me like a lot of billable hours."

"The legal system is not inexpensive and the costs add up very quickly. That's why you may want to consider letting me offer ten thousand to settle with a view to settling for fifteen."

"Fifteen thousand dollars? Never. On principle alone."

"I've got to be honest with you," says Pioche. "A lot of principled people go broke fighting lawsuits."

"But I never infringed anyone's copyright! This is a travesty, an abomination! We should countersue them."

"For what?"

"For wrongful action—for extortion. You're the lawyer, you tell me.""

"By that time, you'll have bills exceeding a hundred thousand dollars if it results in a trial."

"This is unbelievable."

"Welcome to my world. I've thought about giving up the law and getting a job at Starbucks."

"Why don't you?"

"Because I'm too stuck in. I have a wife with serious spending habits, and two kids in private schools…"

Their call ends and Lathom goes deep into a brood.

Jasmine says quietly, "Whatever problem you are experiencing, try not to think about it."

Lathom scoffs. "Easy for you to say, young lady. You're not the one being led to an abattoir." He shakes his head. "Goddamn legal system. Get stung by that bug, you're allergic for life."

"You're already giving your enemy exactly what they want," says Jasmine.

"And what's that?"

"They've invaded your thoughts for the purpose of rattling you. And you've let them in."

"I didn't ask for this."

"Yet you allow the invasion to continue by constantly thinking about it, aggravating yourself and letting it interfere with living your life in the moment."

Lathom waves her off and glares through the windshield at the road ahead.

"Let me ask you something," says Jasmine. "Is there anything more you can do about the situation *right now?*"

He ignores her.

"You don't have to think about the negative situation in which you find yourself if you don't want to. Thinking about it over and over again won't change anything. You might as well put it out of your mind until the next event when you *have* to deal with it. And after dealing with it during the moments you must, discard it again from your mind."

Lathom's phone rings. Conscious that he's being listened to by his fellow road warriors, he shields the phone to conduct a hushed conversation for a couple minutes before disconnecting and resuming his brood.

"What was that about?" asks Blythe.

Lathom harrumphs. "Do I ask you about your private conversations?"

Silence.

"Okay, if you must know, it was an acquaintance of mine from Montecito. T.C. Boyle. He has a mudslide update."

"What mudslide?" asks Jasmine.

Lathom turns. "Don't you watch the news?"

"I try my best not to because…"

"It invades your thoughts?"

"Exactly!" says Jasmine. "I'm glad you're finally seeing this."

"Whether I see it or not, the news is this: *Mother Nature* is trying to get rid of everyone—and for good reason."

"What reason?"

"Humanity is a cancer slowly killing the healthy cell it lives on—planet Earth—with plastic and fumes. Mother Nature's arsenal for curing the human plague is mudslides, tsunamis, tornadoes and volcanoes."

"That's very cynical."

"Take it up with Mother Nature, ma'am, not me."

"Smudge yourself."

"Excuse me?"

"With sage. With any luck, it might purify your thinking." She looks at Blythe. "Hey, mind if I play a CD?"

"I suppose not," says Blythe. "As long as it's not heavy metal or rap."

"Ditto," says Lathom.

Jasmine plucks a CD from her purse and passes it to Blythe for insertion.

The most heavenly music fills the car.

"What is it?" asks Blythe.

"*Miracles.*"

"Excuse me?"

"That's what it's called," says Jasmine, studying Scallywag. "It's from a pianist named Paul Cardall, one of my favorites. "Why does he never move?"

"Who?" asks Lathom.

"Your bearded dragon."

"They eat and poop. And stare," says Lathom. "Not much else. I appreciate their inertia."

A car coming up from behind, doing eighty-plus miles an hour, first flashes, then honks, even though changing lanes would mean having to brake behind a slow-moving truck. When Blythe overtakes the truck and changes lanes, the driver from behind whizzes by and flips Blythe the bird.

"Jeez, can you believe that guy?"

"You haven't walked in his shoes," says Jasmine. "He's probably in need of a blessing. Best thing to do is wish him well."

21.

AFTER much too long on I-5, straight as a pencil and known as The Grapevine, snowcapped Mount Shasta comes into view, first as fleeting glimpses through canyon passes and cloud, but soon unveiled in all its majesty.

Jasmine bounces around the backseat with excitement as they roll nearer.

Seeing a hillside of sheep, Blythe blurts a baa-ing sound—and blushes with embarrassment.

"Sweet," says Jasmine. "You talk to sheep?"

"Aboiment," says Lathom.

"Huh?" She looks at him quizzically.

"You're not a feminist, are you?" asks Lathom.

"Just another label," she replies.

"Good. Then you won't be angry that Blythe's syndrome is not called *a-girl-ment*."

"A what?"

"He makes animal sounds when he sees animals," says Lathom. "Says he can't help it."

Blythe, embarrassed by being outed, says nothing, but exits at the quaint town of Dunsmuir because, by now, two-thirty in the afternoon, all three travelers are famished, especially Lathom who hadn't eaten breakfast and his grumbling tummy is audible enough for all to hear.

The Cornerstone Café, a cheerful slice of Americana, seems a good fit—and good thing since it is the only restaurant open.

Lathom and Blythe order cheeseburgers; Jasmine, being vegan, orders a salad. When their dishes arrive she asks permission to say a blessing and rolls into one before anyone can object.

"Thank you, sunshine, thank you cloud, thank you, farmer. Thank you, cosmos, for coming together to provide healthy and delicious nourishment."

Jasmine proceeds to eat mindfully, chewing slower than the others, remaining quiet, immersed in olfaction and flavor.

"Shasta Abbey is just off the Five," she says, emerging from her trance.

"Huh?" says Lathom.

"The monastery I'd like to see. It's only twelve miles north of here."

Blythe checks his watch. "We've still got another hour and forty minutes to Ashland so it'll have to be brief."

Lathom shakes his head with disdain at the reminder of their destination. "Ass-land."

"No worries," says Jasmine. "I just need to check out the abbey, see if it's the right fit for a longer stay."

"Why do you need a monastery?" asks Lathom. "You could just as easily visit a national park for solitude."

"Because I'm hoping a yoga master will help me create the perfect mantra for myself."

"Oh, I see," Lathom smirks. "I once knew Alan Watts, from my houseboat days. He lived in Sausalito too. Alan used to describe existence with two words: *suchness and thatness*. How about *that* for a mantra? Suchness and thatness. To which I'd add, *thusness*."

Jasmine looks above Lathom 's head. "Give him time, he'll get it," she says sweetly.

Lathom looks up, down and around. "Who are you talking to?"

"Your guardian angel."

"Gee, thanks. Ask him where he's been the last few days. Better yet, ask him where he's been my whole life."

"Has it been that bad?" she asks.

Lathom doesn't answer.

She follows up with another question. "What do you want your last words to be?"

"Is that a threat?"

"No, I'd really like to know."

"You mean my epitaph?" says Lathom. "Easy. *I miss me*."

"Not your epitaph. Your very last words before your journey onward."

"Onward where?"

"The next phase."

"Ah. Of course," says Lathom. "Non-existence. How about, *Sweet dreams?*"

"Good," says Jasmine. "I like that. Mine are, *Hello I'm here.*" She pauses. "And you, Blythe?"

"*The grandson also rises.*"

Lathom raises an eyebrow. "A take on Hemingway?"

Blythe chuckles, a joke between himself and the universe.

22.

Back inside the car, they quickly rejoin I-5 and roll alongside the magical mountain.

Jasmine is in her glory, ooh-ing and ahh-ing and taking photos with her smart phone.

"It's better than I ever imagined," she gushes. "I'm in heaven."

Lathom, preoccupied with his own thoughts, glances at the mountain.

"Mother Nature's invitation," he pronounces caustically, "to an avalanche."

"That's our exit!" Jasmine points excitedly. "Abrams Lake Road—then take a right onto Summit Drive."

Blythe ramps off and follows Jasmine's navigation.

Within a few minutes and a couple of turns, a two-sided gate looms up with the words *Shasta Abbey* in red paint upon granite stone.

As if by magic, the gates swing open—and our trio of visitors roll up into a carport.

Jasmine alights and fills her lungs with very fresh, chilly air.

Blythe and Lathom climb out for a look around and to stretch their muscles. Blythe is about to say something but Jasmine stops him.

"Shh! Listen!"

After a few seconds, Lathom says, "I don't hear a damn thing."

"Exactly," says Jasmine. "Total silence. Very rare."

No sound whatever.

"What you're hearing is the voice of God," Jasmine whispers.

She removes her On Cloud sneakers and prances off barefoot toward an open-air stupa, pausing briefly to lean back and breathe it all in before entering one of the modest wooden structures within this eerily quiet compound of stillness and contemplation.

Fifteen minutes later, reseated at the wheel of his stationary vehicle, Blythe checks and rechecks the time on his phone, stroking his face.

"Nervous?" says Lathom.

"If I don't get us to the gig on time, my ass is grass." Blythe pauses. "Aren't you concerned?"

Lathom shrugs, smiling. "Doesn't matter to me one way or the other. To quote Jasmine, *I'm exactly where I'm supposed to be*. I could care less if we don't make it to Ass-land in time—and since *I'm here*, with *you* in charge of logistics, I am well within the terms of my contract."

Blythe gulps, more nervous than before with the realization that it's all on him. He opens the door. "I'll go get her."

Ten minutes later he returns. Alone.

"She's staying here?" asks Lathom.

"I don't know." Blythe leans forward, hands on his knees, speaking to his passenger through the open car window. "I couldn't find her," he exasperates. "And there's no one around to ask."

"So, let's go."

"Leave Jasmine here?"

"Would serve her right—you told her to be quick, you need to be somewhere."

Blythe shuffles his feet. "I dunno. Can't just leave her here, she's my boss's niece. That could cause me even worse grief."

"The definition of dilemma." Lathom chuckles at Blythe's predicament. "Damned if you do, damned if you don't."

Blythe squints. "Aren't writers supposed to avoid clichés?"

"Touché," says Lathom. "Smartass."

"I guess I'll go take another look around, get some exercise."

Lathom climbs out to stretch his own legs once again.

In the distance, Mount Shasta protrudes from a forest of fir trees beneath a flawless blue sky.

Lost in the moment, Lathom stands transfixed. He doesn't even hear Blythe coming up from behind.

"Are you actually smiling?" asks Blythe.

"Just checking out the mountain," says Lathom. "It's awful pretty out here. Did you find her?"

Blythe shakes his head. "Damndest thing. I can't find *anyone*."

"She couldn't have just disappeared."

"I tried every building." Blythe consults his phone once again. "If we don't get moving soon, we're not going to make it on time."

Lathom shrugs. "Your call."

"Call, call!"

"Is that your aboiment thing?" Lathom glances around. "I don't see any crows anywhere."

"No, no, no. I have her cell number in my contacts. I should *call* it." He taps his phone, which produces a funky melody ever so faintly in the distance.

"It's coming from the car," he says, hopefully. But when he reaches there, with Lathom not far behind, all he finds is Jasmine's phone by itself on the backseat.

"Great," he says with sarcasm. "She left her phone in the car."

Lathom laughs, shaking his head in delight over a new thought.

"What's funny?"

"You kidding? It's probably against company policy for that awful woman to provide transport for her niece at the publisher's expense. If I don't make it on time to the bookstore, they'll want to know why. When you tell them Francine's niece was on the road with us, that she disappeared, and we had to look for her and *that's* why we missed the event, well, that's not going to go down too well for Madam Fassbender, is it?"

"Or me."

"Don't you see? That punctilious bitch can't get rid of you because if you blow the whistle on her for mixing her personal life with business she'll wind up with egg all over her face."

"Really?"

"Really, truly."

"No, I meant *really, another cliché?*"

Just then, Jasmine reappears, practically skipping toward them, a wide smile across her face.

"Wow, that was awesome!" she enthuses.

"Where were you?" asks Blythe.

"I managed to get a meeting with one of the senior monks. He asked me a lot of questions and I guess he liked my answers because he invited me to return and stay for a week whenever I want!"

"I'm happy for you," says Blythe. "But we're way behind schedule. We gotta go, right now."

"That's the spirit!" Jasmine gushes in her exuberance. *"Right now."*

23.

THE first sign of trouble comes from a flashing electronic road sign: *ACCIDENT AHEAD BE PREPARED TO STOP.*

Blythe smacks his steering wheel, truly aggrieved by this unexpected threshold guardian.

"I knew it!" he erupts. "Now we'll never get there on time."

Lathom smirks.

Says Jasmine, "It cannot be otherwise."

"Say that again?" asks Blythe, with an edge.

"It cannot be otherwise."

"What is that supposed to mean?"

"It's self-explanatory," says Jasmine. "As in, it was always meant to be."

"It *could* have been otherwise," snaps Blythe, "if you hadn't taken so long at the monastery. We'd have been *ahead* of that accident, not behind it, and gotten to my author's gig on time."

"Could-have-beens are a waste of time," says Jasmine.

"Yeah, right—as long as you got what *you* wanted."

"Gratitude," says Jasmine.

"That's the best you can offer? No apology?"

"If we'd left when you wanted, it might have been *us* involved in that accident up ahead. If you really want to do coulda-woulda-shoulda, I might have saved our lives."

Lathom weighs in, shaking his head with a sigh. "Do you always rationalize inconsideration?"

Jasmine ponders this.

Lathom turns to Blythe. "Let no good deed go unpunished."

"*Another* cliché?" says Blythe.

"Talking in clichés is okay," says Lathom. "It's *writing* them that's *verboten*."

Sure enough, traffic soon slows to a standstill. And twenty minutes later they are still no further.

Blythe fidgets and huffs.

Jasmine meditates in silence with her eyes closed.

And Lathom naps... until his phone whistles.

"We're in trouble now," he announces in mock alarm to the others after recognizing the 212 area code. "It's the suits at Mulberry calling."

Blythe groans.

Jasmine doesn't stir from her trance.

Lathom answers to a barrage of babble that no one else can hear.

"Yes, that's true," the author says, "but it's unwarranted." He listens some more. "It's under control," he squeezes in edgewise, continuing to listen until another opening. "No. I didn't even know about this until two days ago."

"And you didn't think it necessary to fill us in?" thunders publicity chief Francine Fassbender so loud that the others in the car can hear even though the phone isn't on speaker mode.

"That's my aunt!" chirps Jasmine. "Hi, Aunt Francine!"

"It's not important," Lathom continues his conversation. "Just a frivolous legal matter."

"Well, it may be just a frivolous matter to you," hollers Francine. "But to my publishing house it translates to embarrassment and, more importantly, lost sales. As in dollars and cents."

"Why?"

"Bad publicity!" she shrills. "This kind of thing can kill a book!"

"I had no control over this," says Lathom. "And I never did anything wrong. Does the mere filing of a lawsuit make me guilty until proven innocent?"

"Don't you get it?" says Francine. "It makes you look bad—and, by extension, it makes Mulberry Press look bad."

"The people behind this ridiculous lawsuit know that," Lathom says in exasperation. "That's why they've chosen this window of time to file it. You're falling right into their trap."

"I'm not falling into any trap!" hollers Francine. "I'm responding to a bad situation that *you* are responsible for!"

"That's what I'm trying to tell you—I'm *not* responsible!"

"You can say that again," says Francine. "You're the most *irresponsible* author I've ever had to put up with."

"Do you always end your sentences with a preposition?" says Lathom. "Now I understand why the marketing copy was so poorly constructed."

"How dare you! And don't change the subject!"

"It is what it is," says Lathom. "Or, as your niece is fond of saying…" he winks at Jasmine, "it cannot be otherwise."

"Don't you dare quote my niece to me!"

"No?" says Lathom. "I'll let The Snitch speak for herself."

He passes the phone to a wide-eyed Jasmine, who takes the phone and assures her aunt that all is well and she had a great time at the monastery she'd wanted to visit. She hands the phone back to Lathom, who disconnects Francine without resuming their conversation.

Lathom's face is red with fury as he huffs at Jasmine. "See, I was right—you *are* here to spy on me for that Wicked Witch of the East *and* West."

"I have no idea what you're talking about." Jasmine shakes her head, mildly distressed by this accusation.

"So, you deny it? Such mendacity. You listened to the conversation I had earlier with my lawyer and reported it to Francine. I bet that's why we couldn't find you at the monastery."

"Before you continue speaking," says Jasmine, "ask yourself this question: will your words improve the silence?"

"Admit it," Lathom presses.

"Mister Lathom…" starts Blythe.

"You butt out of it. I'm speaking to Aunt Francine's little spy."

"I'm not a spy."

"Mister Lathom…"

"What?" he snaps at Blythe.

"Jasmine's cell phone was in the car the whole time at the monastery—remember?"

Lathom considers this. "So what? She left her cell to cover her tracks and used someone else's phone."

Jasmine giggles.

"What's so damn funny?"

"Phones aren't permitted inside the monastery compound. The monks aren't permitted to own them and visitors aren't allowed to bring them in."

"How do you know this? Did you *try* to use one?"

"No, I read it on their website. That's why I left mine in the car."

"Then you must have called your aunt from that diner in Dunsmuir."

"No, I didn't." She pauses and holds up her phone. "If you check *recent calls* you'll see I haven't made any today."

Lathom studies the screen. "Doesn't prove anything—you could have deleted it. How else could your aunt have found out? And the timing? The bitch she is, she was willing to throw her own niece under the bus."

"Believing what you want, and repeating it over and over again, doesn't make it true," says Jasmine.

"Is that the mantra you discovered for yourself at the monastery?" Lathom taunts. "How about something simpler, like, *I Spy?*"

Jasmine opens the car door and alights into stationary traffic.

"Hey!" calls Blythe. "Where are you going?"

Jasmine walks a few steps and turns to face the sun, on its final descent toward the horizon. She stands looking directly at it for about thirty seconds, then climbs back into the car.

"I thought you took off," says Blythe, relieved.

Jasmine chuckles. "Why would I do that on an interstate in the middle of nowhere?"

Blythe shrugs. "What *were* you doing?"

"Staring at the sun."

"Why?"

"The sun stimulates the pineal gland, the spirit molecule I told you about earlier. Mystics in India do it every day to stop their pineal from calcifying."

"But isn't looking at the sun dangerous for your eyes?"

Jasmine shakes her head. "That's what everyone is taught to believe. But it's a myth."

"It won't burn your retina and blind you?" asks Blythe, incredulous.

"It's all about timing," says Jasmine. "Yes, it's dangerous to look at the sun most of the time because of ultraviolet rays. But the sun does not give off ultraviolet rays within one hour of sunrise or within one hour of sunset. As long as you stick to those hours, you can look directly at the sun and absorb its energy. The key is to start with ten seconds, and increase each day, progressively, ten seconds each day. If you miss a day, start over, back to ten seconds."

Lathom crosses his arms. "Why take the risk?"

"After staring at the sun, I close my eyes and see God. You should try it sometime, it's very inspirational."

"Literal enlightenment?" says Lathom, tongue-in-cheek.

"Exactly." Jasmin nods. "It may even be what mystics partly mean by *seeing the light*." She fiddles with her phone. "It inspired me to figure out the answer to how my aunt knows about whatever Chris thinks I overheard.

Here," she addresses Lathom, passing her phone to him. "Look at this."

Lathom studies the screen and reads. Then his jaw drops, mouth agape.

The Wikipedia page in his name has an addendum since he last viewed it some time ago; a new concluding section labeled "Controversy," which details the allegations of the lawsuit filed in Federal Court against him for copyright infringement.

"Sonofabitch!" he hollers.

"Did you really steal somebody's photograph?" asks Jasmine, grinning.

"No, I did not," says Lathom, seething.

"In that case, time for Wu Wei."

"Wu *what?*"

"In Taoism, Wu Wei means non-doing."

"No-doing what?"

"Non-doing anything in reaction to whatever negativity is sent your way demanding a reaction."

"And how am I supposed to do that?"

"Like this: be mindful that you have free will over how to respond to external circumstances. You may choose to let anything and everything pass through you without a response. If you need a physical reaction, shrug it off, like a duck flapping its wings after a tiff with another duck. Let the bad feeling go, just let it go, and move on with something positive in mind—or even better, a completely clear mind."

She pauses before filling the silence. "One of the things I learned back at the monastery is that at any given time, we all, each one of us, have eighty-three problems."

"Only eighty-three?" says Lathom, a hint of sarcasm.

"Precisely eighty-three. That's what a Zen master told me. And if you solve one, it gets replaced by another."

She pauses. "You know what the eighty-fourth problem is?"

"I don't," says Lathom. "And I can hardly wait for you to tell me."

"The eighty-fourth problem is wanting all your problems to go away."

Finally, traffic begins to move.

"See?" says Jasmine. "Positive thinking leads to positive results."

"We're already screwed," says Blythe, so upset he looks like he's on the verge of tears. "We'll never get there on time." He glances at Lathom. "Maybe you should phone the bookstore, explain our predicament?"

"Me? None of this *predicament* is *my* fault. You're in charge of getting me where I'm supposed to be—and Jasmine held us up in Shasta. She may not be a *spy* but she's certainly responsible for this debacle."

"I would hardly call this a debacle," laughs Jasmine.

Lathom turns to face her. "I borrowed that word from your aunt. She used it first. Do you like *hugger-mugger of a book tour* any better?""

"Not really."

"Then what would *you* call it?"

"Part of the magic that's all around us while we deal with human time constraints."

"Easy for you," Blythe laments. "My job *depends* on human time constraints."

"*Just Blythe*, has a point," says Lathom. "Maybe you're not a spy, but you are quite likely a *saboteur*."

"A what?"

"You certainly sabotaged tonight's event. How much is your splenetic aunt paying you for this?"

"My *what* aunt?"

"Spiteful."

"You guys are ridiculous." Jasmine waves them off.

"Well, if your aunt isn't paying you, she's not going to be happy when she hears it's *your* fault we didn't arrive on time."

"You'd tell her that?"

"Why wouldn't I?" scoffs Lathom. "It's true."

"So that makes *you* the snitch, not me—right? Okay, what's the name of the bookstore? I'll handle this."

"Bloomsbury Books," says Blythe.

She accesses their number and hits *call*.

"Hello, my name is Jasmine and I'm the personal assistant to Mister Christopher Lathom, *esteemed* author." She glances at him with a scrunched face. "We have been caught in traffic due to an accident on I-5 and, I'm sorry to say, we're running late for this evening's book event."

Jasmine listens to the voice on the other end.

"Can you please say that again?"

Jasmine hits the speaker key.

"We don't have anything scheduled for this evening," says a female voice, for all to hear. "Maybe you're thinking of Tree House Books up the street?"

"Thank you."

Jasmine connects to Tree House Books.

No. Nothing planned.

"You see," says Jasmine with a big smile. "It wasn't supposed to be." She pauses. "OMG!"

Lathom turns to study here. "Did you really just say 'OMG?' Who *does* that?"

"Where is that stink coming from?" Jasmine pinches her nose.

"Jesus!" says Blythe. "I smell it, too."

Lathom chuckles. "You saw Scallywag eat and stare. Now you get to experience that third thing. It can be pretty vile," he adds, an understatement.

All windows are duly lowered and Blythe ramps off at the next exit for a bearded dragon poop clean-up and air freshener for the car.

**

Back on the road, our traveling trio see up close what the hold-up was: A sixteen-wheeler truck had jackknifed and overturned, destroying two other vehicles in the process.

An ambulance and assorted police cruisers were still on the scene.

"Coulda been us," says Jasmine, looking around in awe at the carnage.

Lathom smirks. "Thought you didn't do coulda beens?"

She smirks. "Now who's the wise-ass?"

24.

THE sun has long since set, dusk turned to dark, when they roll into the center of Ashland.

"Wow!" Jasmine thrills. "What amazing colors!"

Two hundred and two species of indigenous trees in full autumnal color—magentas, burgundies and golden tallow— are indeed a spectacle to behold, even in darkness beneath the light of a three-quarter waxing moon.

Lathom looks around, offers his own perspective. "I'd call it deciduous."

Jasmine chuckles.

"Not gorgeous? Never mind, I'll look it up. Wow—look at that?"

A vintage Volkswagen minibus painted in psychedelic colors is parked on the side of the road, its owner hawking tie-dyed shirts.

"I'm going to buy one of those!" she enthuses.

"It's the Sixties come back to haunt us," muses Lathom.

Blythe winds around to the parking lot of the Ashland Springs Hotel and officiously checks everyone into rooms.

Upstairs, Lathom splashes water on his face and, giving up (again) on the television remote, he descends to Lark, on the hotel's ground floor, settling upon a stool at a long bar softly illuminated by art deco table lamps—a 1930s style that suits his sensibilities.

It is already past eight o'clock.

Good thing there had been no book signing event, as they would have missed it entirely. Lathom is unsure whether to be annoyed or delighted by the scheduling screw-up. Let Casamigos Reposado tequila decide—make it a double.

Blythe and Jasmine had disappeared to their respective rooms, causing Lathom to make a mental note about whether or not Francine was billing her niece's room to the company.

Mostly, Lathom is tired, feeling almost whimsical.

Road fever.

It's funny how sitting all day in a moving vehicle can tire a person out, maybe the downside of stimulating the brain with motion and passing scenery. Or maybe it was the spirited banter he'd had with Jasmine, a youngster with a zest for finding true meaning in life, which, at least to himself, he found admirable, if somewhat pointless.

Lathom is into his second pour of Casamigos, looking across the restaurant to Main Street through plate glass, when Blythe and Jasmine round into the bar. On one hand, the author is enjoying time alone; on the other, he is happy to see them again—not that he would ever admit to it—a special bond that often comes among fellow road-trippers.

"Mind if we join you?" asks Blythe.

"It's a free country. Actually, it's not as free as they'd like you to think. But certainly free enough for you to sit wherever you'd like."

Blythe and Jasmine grab barstools on either side of Lathom.

"We decided that after this *de-ba-cle*," Jasmine enunciates, "you might want company."

"How so?"

"You're a famous author," says Blythe. "You shouldn't be treated this way."

He shrugs. "I've been treated worse. And I'm *glad* there was no event tonight."

"Why?" says Jasmine.

"Because I loathe book signings, that's why."

"Would you like to try some Lithia water?"

Lathom studies the shelves behind the bar. "Is that a cocktail or something?"

"No. It's a natural mineral found in the water here. Ashland is famous for it."

He squints with one eye, suspicious of what he's getting into. "Why?"

"You've heard of Lithium—the drug that psychiatrists use to treat bipolar syndrome?" She holds up a plastic bottle she'd filled earlier from a public well at Lithia Park, within walking distance of the hotel. "This is the original potion. Native Americans called it *Holy Water* because of its curative powers. Try some—it might improve your disposition."

"There's nothing wrong with my disposition, young lady."

She chuckles.

The bartender overhearing, offers a glass.

Jasmine pours.

Lathom swirls it around, sniffs and tastes—and gags, before spitting it across the bar.

"Mawkish!" He wipes his mouth and tongue.

"Like rotten eggs!"

"True," Jasmine concedes. "In addition to Lithia, the local water has Sulfur in it, which spoils the flavor. But the upside is, drinking Lithia water makes people very calm. This is why Ashlantis is such a peaceful place. Sometimes I think the world's whole drinking supply should be spiked with Lithia water. It's probably the only way to end war and bring about world peace." She pauses. "By the way, I'd like to apologize for making us late."

"It didn't matter, even if there had been an event," says Lathom.

"I'm sorry anyway—we would have gotten here a lot sooner and not been stuck in the car so long."

"Thank you, young lady. Apology accepted."

"And I'm sorry you have to take this trip when you don't want to."

"No need for you to be sorry about that." He toasts the air with tequila. "Here's to the next *de-ba-cle.*"

"We'll get an earlier start," says Blythe. "Give ourselves plenty of time."

"Hardly matters to me," says Lathom. "But just out of curiosity, were you able to find out who screwed up tonight's event?"

"I tried," says Blythe. "The office is closed and Francine's cell went to voicemail." Blythe pulls the crumpled itinerary from a pocket and studies it. "Oh shit," he mumbles.

"What is it?" asks Jasmine.

"*I'm* the culprit." Blythe smacks his forehead. "We're supposed to do Bloomsbury Books on the *way back*."

Lathom sighs. "Well, at least we know that nobody screwed up."

"I did. Sorry, Mister Lathom."

"Quit saying *sorry*, both of you, so I may tell you the saddest book tour story I ever heard. If you're interested."

"I am," says Blythe.

"Me, too."

"I used to know a gentleman named Livingston Biddle—you've heard of the Biddles of Philadelphia? Suffice to say, a very prominent family. His first novel, which was published in 1950 by Julian Messner was aptly titled Main Line, and was slated to be a bestseller. That's how things truly work in the book publishing business, in case you didn't know, most people don't. It's all based on literary politics and, more especially, money. How much a publisher is willing to put into a book, to spend.

"Anyway, it was predetermined that Liv Biddle's book

would be big, really big, because the powers that be in the book world would *make* it big. Part of that was a lengthy nationwide book tour that would launch, on publication day, at Brentano's in Beverly Hills.

"So, there's Biddle, at the age of thirty-two, on the cusp of becoming a huge literary star with promise of fame, riches, movie deals—the whole shebang. He arrives the day before the book signing, they've booked him into the swank Beverly Wilshire Hotel, and he's so excited he decides to take an evening stroll up Beverly Drive to Little Santa Monica Boulevard, to Brentano's, after hours, to see the window book his publisher promised would be huge."

Lathom pauses. "And you know what he finds?"

Blythe shrugs.

"Tell us," says Jasmine.

"There's a Biddle book in the window—hundreds of copies. But it's not Liv's novel. You know what happened?"

Both his listeners are riveted.

"That season, Julian Messner also published the memoirs of Francis Biddle, who was Treasury Secretary to Roosevelt—and Liv's cousin."

Lathom pauses. "They'd shipped the wrong Biddle. Everywhere. Book tour cancelled. As a result, Francis Biddle's book became a bestseller and Liv's novel was quickly forgotten, his literary career crushed by a clerical error."

Dinner, this night, is at the bar: Organic field greens for Jasmine; southern fried chicken breast for her two companions.

"Let's make this a feast-forward," says Jasmine.

"A what?" says Lathom.

"It's a celebration."

"Celebrating *what?*" asks Lathom.

"We don't know yet," says Jasmine. "We're manifesting something special to happen down the road."

"This road trip?"

"Not necessarily. The road of life. That's why it's called a feast-*forward*."

Lathom harrumphs.

Jasmine raises her glass of Lithia water. "Tonight, we celebrate a future event, thus far unknown, but an event that will, one day soon, make us all very happy."

Fried chicken, mashed potatoes and collard greens—as comfortable a dish as comfort food can be—is mightily quaffed down by the two men while Jasmine loses her senses to a salad of toasted hazelnuts and dried cranberries.

"I'm tired," she says, after cleaning her plate. "I'm going to take a hot bath and crash."

Blythe nods goodbye, but stays put. "Is it okay," he says hesitantly to Lathom, "if I bounce an idea for a novel off you?"

"Shoot."

"It's called *Flipped*."

"Good title. As long as it's not about dolphins. I hate stories about dolphins."

"No, no dolphins. It's about a couple who meet and begin to fall in love. But then the guy discovers he's more attracted to men while at the same time the girl decides she's more attracted to women."

"So far, very modern Hollywood—they'll love it. Go on."

"They break up, go their own ways. Each, on their own, decides to undergo transgender surgery. Pretty soon after that they meet again by accident—and fall in love all over again, this time for real." He pauses, watching Lathom's face for a reaction.

Lathom remains stone-faced.

"What do you think?"

"I think I'll have another drink. By myself."

And Lathom is left alone with his thoughts, which are mostly about why he ever bothered to publish a second novel.

Back inside his room, Lathom is determined to master the TV remote—or at least turn on the news or a late-night comedy show.

The television, though, has other ideas, perhaps even a digital mind of its own, because he can hardly get beyond a welcoming screen that spells out his last name and when he does, the screen fills with a batch of hotel services. And beyond that, a portal for in-room movies at $9.99 each.

"Goddam it!" Lathom finally hollers, flinging the remote across the room. "Whatever happened to seven channels—and news that presented just the facts ma'am!"

PART THREE

25.

NEXT morning.

Blythe is ready to roll.

So is Jasmine.

But Lathom's absence is pronounced; he is nowhere to be found.

After knocking on his door for third time, Blythe cultivates a bad feeling about this. He consults reception, which in turn consults housekeeping, which sends a maid accompanied by Blythe to Lathom's room.

The maid knocks twice, to no avail. She inserts a key card into the lock.

Blythe braces himself for the worst.

The door swings inward.

The room is empty.

No Lathom. And none of Lathom's belongings, either.

Just plain empty.

"Shit-squared," mutters Blythe, dashing downstairs to enquire about public transportation for getting out of town. The most likely way out—maybe the *only* way out, southbound, he learns, is Greyhound's once daily 12:35 p.m. bus to San Fran.

Blythe pinpoints the station on his phone map—between Stratford Inn and Ashland Cemetery—and, along with Jasmine and all their gear, drives straight there, double-parks, jumps out and dashes into the station.

Sure enough, Lathom is sitting inside, his travel bag at his feet.

When the author sees Blythe coming through the entrance, he tries to shrink himself into his hat and safari vest, but the jig is clearly up.

"Where are you going?" asks Blythe.

"Got myself a ticket to Fog City," says Lathom, part sheepish, part like it's the most natural thing in the world.

"Was my story idea that bad?" asks Blythe.

Lathom chuckles.

The ice is broken.

"We're supposed to drive to Portland," says Blythe. "Remember?"

Part of Blythe isn't sure if Lathom isn't suffering from early Alzheimer's, such is the author's expression of indifference.

"I'm sorry, young man, I've had enough. I just can't do anymore of this book tour nonsense. Time to abrogate."

Blythe sits behind him and wrings his hands. He does not want to fail. And at this point, he does not want to see Lathom fail, either.

"Sorry, I know I should have told you," Lathom continues. "But I didn't decide until this morning. I woke up early after a bad night's sleep. And after two cups of coffee I felt compelled to break free. That book drive did me in."

"This tour?"

"No, the book drive at that school in Napa Valley. Seeing all that desuetude."

Blythe laughs. "Desue-what?"

"In my case, those discarded books." He shivers. "Including mine." He looks up at Blythe with mournful eyes "I just don't know what the point is anymore."

"I understand how you feel," says Blythe, having considered the matter on the short drive over. "But please listen to my reasoning."

Lathom remains silent.

"It makes a lot more sense *logistically* for you to come to Portland with us then to depart like this," Blythe explains. "Do the math. It'll take you twelve hours to reach San Francisco by bus—and then you're still not home. But in less than five hours we'll be in Portland and you can take a nonstop flight from PDX to Santa Barbara.

"It's practically a no-brainer."

Lathom nods. "I understand. But I thought I might use the opportunity of being in Frisco to try and find that gal I once knew."

"Who?"

"My Sausalito sweetheart, the gal I lived with on a houseboat who made great coffee and blueberry pancakes."

"Oh," Blythe smiles, stumped.

"But, you know, you're right," says Lathom. "Twelve hours on a bus is not very enticing when I can get home more easily by going to Portland." He stands and picks up his bag.

"May I take that for you?" Blythe is amazed, and greatly relieved, by how well his pitch worked. But it truly did make the most sense from a logistical standpoint.

"Thank you. My back hurts."

Blythe catches a whiff of Lathom. "Jeez, do you ever bathe?"

The author smirks indignantly. "I take a shower once a week, whether I need one or not."

As they approach the car, Jasmine leans out the front passenger seat window. "Trying to ditch me? I can understand that. But what about poor Scallywag?"

Lathom climbs into the backseat and checks on his bearded dragon, who looks him directly in the eye, as if to say, *how dare you try to desert me.*

"Blythe would have brought him home to me—right, Blythe?"

Blythe grunts and ignites the car—and off they go, a short drive to the interstate, during which he takes a call from Francine, tells her he figured out Ashland was on the rebound, sorry for the confusion, otherwise all is well and they're headed for Portland.

Lathom sits quietly, gazing out the window, hypnotized by the motional blur of passing scenery—green and clean, ignoring the odd call on his phone and shifting occasionally to ease the pain emanating from his right buttock.

About halfway up, near Eugene, they roll into a service station for gas (pumped by an attendant, no self-service, Oregon law) and Fritos, beef jerky and Snickers bars for the men and raw nuts and trial mix for Jasmine, who also uses the stop to replenish herself with flouride-free bottled water.

"Road food," hoots Blythe.

"You're awfully quiet," says Jasmine to Lathom, after a long spell of quiet herself.

The author shakes his head. "I woke up with pain in my lower back and it's been shooting down my right leg. It definitely does not enhance sociability."

"Is it like a sharp knife or a dull ache?" asks Jasmine.

"Both. More like a knife, I guess."

"It's your sciatic nerve," Jasmine diagnoses. "I doubt you pulled anything."

"That's a relief."

"Not really. Pulling something is easier to treat, with rest, cold compresses and a heating pad. Sciatica comes from stress. And once that nerve gets pinched, it's very hard to *un*-pinch."

"Damn lawsuit," mutters Lathom.

"You have to put whatever's bothering you out of your mind," says Jasmine softly. "Deal with it only when you absolutely have to, otherwise don't give it a thought." She pauses. "That's why people need meditation in their lives. It dispels the chattering monkeys in our mind and makes us clearer and aware of our true consciousness."

Lathom studies her skeptically. "You think I can meditate this pain away?"

"You're not supposed to *seek* anything through meditation, that's not what it's for. But it might help with your mental pain."

"I don't *have* mental pain," scoffs Lathom.

"If you say so. Meditation will take you away from the clutter-full thoughts that fill your mind. Disease is *dis-ease*. Ease up on yourself. Relax. And don't allow yourself to worry. Worrying never solves anything, it just spoils the moment."

"Yeah, well right now I need to do something about this pain. Either of you have ibuprofen?"

Whizzing past a town called Albany, Blythe ramps off and finds a 7/11 convenience store.

Lathom hobbles in and buys Advil and a bottle of water and swallows three tabs on the spot.

"I can teach you how to meditate if you like," says Jasmine after they've resumed the drive.

Lathom sighs, hoping the painkiller will cut in soon. "As your captive audience, I guess I have no choice."

"I'd like to learn how to meditate," says Blythe while wondering if maybe his author is faking lower back pain as a precursor to bailing from this book tour.

"Okay, then," says Jasmine. "Begin by straightening your posture. Sit straight up, don't lean back."

Reluctantly, Lathom obliges. "I sure hope you're not going to tell me to close my eyes and chant *Ohm*."

Jasmine shakes her head. "Keep your eyes open and stare straight ahead. Ready?"

"I can't believe I'm doing this," he mutters.

"I want you to start with three long breaths. Inhale with your nose, fill your lungs, exhale slowly through your mouth. Like we did yesterday."

Lathom reluctantly complies.

"Good. Now, breathe normally, through your nose. And as you breathe, focus on your breath and only your breath." She gives him space to proceed. "Is your mind clear?"

"No."

Jasmine chuckles. "Instead of dwelling on your thoughts, just *observe* them."

Lathom opens one eye. "How do I do that?"

"Detach yourself from your thoughts, observe what you're thinking, notice what you notice, and watch your thoughts as if they are passing clouds. Your thoughts are not really yours."

"No?" says Lathom "Whose thoughts are they, then?"

"They are manufactured by your mind to set you apart from everyone else and make your ego central to your existence. And since you interrupted me, and the process, not to mention that you have a much bigger ego than most people, you have to start over."

Blythe chuckles.

Lathom groans.

"Breathe three long breaths," Jasmine continues. "As you breathe, concentrate on your breath. If you must think, think *in, out, in, out,* as you're breathing, because it is difficult for your mind to try to take over and think about other things when you're focused on your breathing *and* thinking *in and out.*"

Lathom follows her instructions. For a few minutes.

"Okay, okay," he says impatiently. "What's next?"

"Nothing's next," says Jasmine. "But if you've had enough, we can make it more interesting. Focus on your senses. One sense at a time. Start with your nose. As you inhale, explore your sense of smell."

At that moment, Blythe unleashes a staccato three-part fart.

Jasmine freezes, mortified. "Are you kidding me?"

Lathom holds his nose, shaking his head. "At least it was an honest fart."

"A what?"

"Nothing sneaky about it."

At first trying to keep a straight face, Blythe bursts into a fit of laughter, mostly due to the author's comment. "C'mon, it's not like you didn't *ask* for that."

Jasmine opens her eyes and shakes her head in disgust. "Not funny." She lowers her window. "Men."

"I think you should report him to Aunt Francine," says Lathom.

Jasmine throws her arms up. "I give up on both of you."

"No, please don't," says Blythe. "I'm sorry."

"I'll have to start from the beginning," says Jasmine.

After running through the rituals of focus, of the senses, she instructs Lathom to choose a word and then focus on that chosen word to the exclusion of all else.

"Don't tell me what the word is," she adds. "Just

choose a word, any word, and focus on it. No talking now. Quiet."

A few minutes pass.

"Okay," says Jasmine. "Now open your eyes and look at everything as if you are a new born baby, all the lights and colors and passing scenery."

Lathom obliges.

"Now, last step, you need to focus your eyes on any object of your choosing. The flame of a candle works well. But since we're in a moving car, we'll do this a different way. Look directly into my eyes." Jasmine twists to face Lathom head-on.

"Is this a blinking contest?" asks Lathom.

"No. You can blink all you want. But don't take your eyes out of mine."

Two minutes of eye-gazing pass.

"Are you trying to hypnotize me?" asks Lathom.

"No, this has nothing to do with hypnosis. Just keep staring into my eyes. Don't think about why. Don't think about anything. Just gaze."

Three minutes pass.

"Are you downloading my brain?" asks Lathom, becoming alarmed.

"Don't be silly," says Jasmine. "What would I do with all the egoic nonsense in your brain?"

Another five minutes pass.

Finally, Jasmine disengages.

Lathom sits back, sighs, relaxes.

"Whoa," he says. "What just happened?"

"Simple," says Jasmine. "I cured your sciatica."

Lathom considers this, moves his leg back and forth, grimaces. "Then how come it still hurts?"

"Baggage. It may take a while for you to understand it's gone before you're able to let it go."

Blythe farts again. "You mean like that?"

"I don't believe you," says Jasmine, waving madly to clear the air.

"Do you believe Hippocrates?" says Blythe. "The father of medicine said it's better to let gas out than hold it in. And after all that road food…"

Lathom laughs heartily, and lets one rip himself—and winces at the pain it causes to his sciatic nerve. "Owwww!"

"Serves you right," says Jasmine.

26.

THEY pull into Stumptown just after three o'clock in the afternoon.

Blythe eases into the valet spot outside The Heathman on SW Broadway, adjacent to an historic theater known as The Schnitz. The theater's vintage marquee, evoking a sense of place, not only captivates Lathom, but causes this lyric to float around his mind, albeit absent of its origin.

We pulled into Portland Town, we been on road.

He points up to the word PORTLAND. "I guess we're here."

And with it, an epiphany of sorts: *Portland Woman,* New Riders of the Purple Sage.

"I'm heading up to the Japanese Garden to lose myself," says Jasmine.

"Always remember," she adds, "stop and smell the roses..."

"Smell the roses?" Lathom glances at Blythe. "And you think *I* talk in clichés?"

"Portland is known for its roses," says Jasmine. "You may not know it, but one of Portland's nicknames is Rose City." She circles around the car to peck Lathom on the cheek.

Her soft lips remind the author of his lost love in Sausalito. But something more than that: an aroma on her that takes him back to his childhood, say, around eight years-old, to Camden, Maine—a one-time summer vacation, the scent of blueberries, and perhaps the scent of his mother—a stirring of his soul that brings an unexpected tear to his right eye, requiring discreet removal and, in the process, rediscovering a sentimental part of himself he thought he'd long ago buried.

"And one last thing, to do with your sciatic nerve flare-up," says Jasmine, turning around, her sympathetic brown eyes connecting with Lathom's. "Don't carry your wallet in your back pocket."

He watches, shaking his head in awe as this scintillating free spirit, duffle bag tucked beneath her right arm; a part of him is sorry to see her go as she prances off beneath a green neon shop sign that says *John Helmer, Haberdasher.*

"I'll be damned," Lathom thinks aloud to himself. "Isn't the word haberdasher outlawed by now?"

Blythe flips the car key to a valet dressed in a teal and gold uniform with a double-breasted coat looking partly like it derives from when the hotel was founded in 1927 and partly as if it were customized for Michael Jackson.

"I feel like I've gone back in time," says Lathom.

"Where's the car going with Scallywag in it?" he asks the valet.

"Parking lot around the corner," the valet replies.

"Be sure to keep a window cracked," says Lathom.

27.

INSIDE the landmark building, while Blythe barks at a couple of pet dogs in the lobby and runs through the hotel's registration process, Lathom wanders into The Heathman Library. He's pleasantly surprised by the floor-to-ceiling bookshelves that rise to a galleried mezzanine, housing more than 3,000 volumes, many of them first editions signed by the author.

"Literary heaven," says Lathom to himself; certainly, a vast improvement to the book drive they had happened upon in Calistoga two days earlier.

Blythe follows him in. "Good to go!" he calls, holding up key cards. "We've got a couple hours before the event. I'm going to take a walk and get coffee. Why don't you rest up and I'll see you in the lobby at five-thirty?"

"Meet me in the bar," says Lathom.

After checking into his room, the author descends and

exits the hotel, crosses Salmon Street and enters—shaking his head in awe—a portal that takes him back in time half-a-century.

Felt hats! Ornate walking sticks! Tartan cashmere scarves! He springs for the latter, a hedge against Rose City's cold and damp weather, and wears it to go, confident it will spare him from catching a cold.

28.

THE Heathman Hotel's bar is part of a separate conces-
sion called Headwaters restaurant. And this is where we find
Lathom, upon a barstool just before five o'clock, minutes
before this popular watering hole fills up with happy hour
revelers.

The first few sips of their specialty cocktail, Vieux Carre
(rye, brandy, vermouth and Benedictine), eases the pain in
Lathom's right buttock. He wishes he could remain in this
spot all evening, in advance of catching a plane home tomorrow, and be done with bookstore events once and for
all.

Blythe rolls in and, with nowhere to sit, squeezes himself
into a stance beside Lathom.

"Phew," he says. "I thought you might have hightailed
for the airport."

"Don't think I didn't consider it," growls Lathom. "But

their one and only daily flight to Santa Barbara departed before we got here. I know, because I checked. But I'm flying out tomorrow," he adds.

Blythe frowns.

"Don't take it personally," continues Lathom. "Not your fault. You did your best to keep this hayride to doom on track. As a consolation, I'll give you an idea for a novel I dreamt up during a nap I just took."

Blythe sips the small craftsman beer delivered to him.

"Hey," Lathom smirks. "I thought you weren't supposed to drink while on driving duty?"

Blythe shrugs sheepish. "This is Portland. Everyone drinks craftsman beer in this town, working or not."

"Doesn't matter to me," says Lathom. "To hell with Mulberry's suits and all their dumb rules. Okay, now, the novel: Your protagonist starts off in a library or a used bookstore. While perusing the travel section he comes across a vintage travel guide—could be any decade or place you want it to be, but do your research and find a real used book store and a genuine travel guide on which to base this story, for verisimilitude's sake."

"Vera who?"

Lathom studies his media escort, unsure if he's being serious or facetious, before continuing. "As a lark, the protagonist decides to take a road trip to the travel guide destination, with the idea of using the old guide as a reference to see what's still there and what isn't, what has changed. You grasp that?"

"Got it."

"But when the protagonist arrives, he slowly discovers that the place is *exactly* as the vintage guide depicts. And why is that? Because he soon finds that the guide is some kind of magical portal that has taken him back in time to the way it was when the guide was first published."

Blythe nods. "I like that genre, magic realism."

"Genre." Lathom shakes his head. "No such thing. It's just a modern invention. There's good writing and bad writing. Good storytelling and bad storytelling. Period."

Blythe takes a final swig of beer and checks the time on his phone. "Better drink up, we may have some rush hour traffic."

Lathom lifts himself off the stool, now feeling no pain at all. "Alcohol," he says. "Best cure for whatever ails you."

29.

THE valet brings the car up and, once inside, Lathom feeds Scallywag some lettuce he scavenged from Headwaters' kitchen. They roll along West Burnside, take a right on NW 23rd, drive through a funky upscale neighborhood of cafes and boutiques and, finally, many blocks later, arrive at New Renaissance Books.

"That's it," says Blythe, pointing at three conjoined turquoise-and-cream-colored craftsman houses, with this sign: *Resources for Growth and Inspiration.*

"What the hell kind of bookstore is this?" says Lathom with irritated bemusement.

Blythe shrugs. "Let's go in and find out."

"Must we?"

After parking around the corner, a residential street, they walk in light drizzle and step up to the bookshop's quaint wooden porch. The first thing Lathom notices is a poster of himself—utilizing the same photo over which he was being sued for copyright infringement.

He groans, and mutters to himself, "My fault, no doubt. Maybe they'll add this bookstore to the lawsuit."

"What's that?" says Blythe.

"Nothing," says Lathom, feeling a twinge of pain in his butt.

Once inside, it appears that New Renaissance is so-named because it is a New Age bookstore, featuring, in addition to mostly self-help and inspirational books, crystals, holistic jewelry, candles and organic shower gel.

"Look at the bright side," Blythe whispers.

"What bright side?"

"At least there's no stuffed rabbits." Blythe sniffles like a bunny at the mere thought.

Lathom does a 360-degree slow-motion twirl, disbelief growing, and then he sees someone... a familiar someone.... "What the...?"

"Hello!" calls Jasmine, prancing over. "I didn't know this was where your book event was until ten minutes ago when I saw your poster in the window! Great choice of venue!"

Lathom rolls his eyes, continuing his survey of the scene around him. "I shouldn't be here. I should be at Powell's."

Jasmine shakes her head. "I already told you—you're exactly where you're supposed to be. By the way, how's your backache?"

Lathom considers this. "I thought I drank it away—until I got here."

Blythe, having gone off to find someone in charge, returns with the bookstore manager—and both of them are somewhat perplexed.

"I'm so sorry," the manager says to Lathom.

"Sorry for what?"

"Your books didn't arrive."

"*What?*"

"Crazy, huh?" She shrugs. "We're supposed to have a book signing—and no books. Never happened before—go figure."

Lathom closes his eyes and shakes his head before turning on Blythe. "The inchoateness of your employer boggles my mind."

"Huh?" says Blythe.

"You're still welcome to talk about your novel," says the manager, mustering enthusiasm. "We'll take orders from customers. You can sign your name on notepad paper and we'll insert your signatures once the books arrive."

Lathom cringes at the thought, wondering what someone might type above his signature, falsely binding him to something or other, resulting in another lawsuit.

"Dare I ask," Lathom addresses Blythe. "Is the frightful Francine Fassbender aware that no books have been delivered here? Or maybe she's *responsible* for it."

Jasmine overhears. "Another *de-ba-cle?*"

Lathom nods.

"Another debacle, indeed."

The bookstore manager takes her guest author by the

hand. "Come with me," she says. "A few of my favorite book readers are very excited to meet you."

Lathom reluctantly follows, looking down at his clasped hand, thinking, *Where the devil is my Purell?*

In another room, a gaggle of gals awaits the author; they titter with minor applause when he enters.

"And someone baked chocolate chip cookies just for you," says the manager with a wide smile.

Much to Lathom's relief, she finally releases his hand.

"Try one." She holds out a tray of freshly baked cookies.

Having not eaten dinner, but only snacked, much earlier on road food, Lathom is famished. He chooses a cookie and gobbles it down, and then masticates another, mingling cordially with his fans while, with desperate eyes, he searches for an exit ramp.

Twenty minutes later, or maybe an hour (he isn't actually sure), Lathom is feeling mellower than when he'd arrived; mellower than before, mellower than ever—and willing to respond to the kind of trivial questions that would normally cause him to roll his eyes or storm out or both.

Even a question about rabbits does not perturb him, but instead provokes an amused chuckle when, as if he were an eight-year-old boy, he puts his hands alongside the top of his head to create rabbit ears, causing Blythe, standing and watching nearby, to break into fits of uncontrollable laughter.

30.

ONCE the author's audience thins out, Lathom and Blythe retreat to nearby Nob Hill Bar & Grill.

The bookstore manager had offered Lathom a free book of his choice—company policy for authors at such events—and he had chosen *1100 Words You Need to Know.*

"Here, this is for you." Lathom hands the paperback to Blythe.

"For me?"

"That's what I just said. Your organon."

"My what?"

"If you want to be a writer, you'll need to improve your vocabulary. From now on, instead of saying *what* or *huh* when I speak a word you don't understand, look it up."

"Thank you," says Blythe, pleasantly surprised by the gift. He flips through the pages. "That's the best argument for cannabis I've ever seen," he adds while awaiting the bartender's attention.

"This book?"

"No, I'm talking about the chocolate chip cookies they fed us."

"What about them?"

"You don't know?"

"Know what?"

"They were *edibles.*"

"Edi…what?"

"They had THC in them."

"THC?"

"Cannabis."

"Pot?" Lathom erupts, disbelieving.

"Exactly."

"No wonder I feel… odd," says Lathom.

"Good odd?"

"I don't know—*odd*-odd."

"How many of those cookies did you eat?"

"Two."

"Whoa!" Blythe shakes his head, grinning widely. "One of those babies is more than enough for me. And you had *two?*"

"I was hungry. I had no idea…"

"I couldn't stop laughing," Blythe interrupts, "when you did your little rabbit imitation. I hope you didn't overdo it."

"How can they put cannabis in cookies and offer them to eat without even telling us?"

"This is Portland," says Blythe. "People here do whatever they want. For these folks, cannabis is like any other spice."

"I was wondering why this beer tastes so good."

From a section of the menu called, appropriately, *Munchies*, Lathom and Blythe order *the ultimate house blend sliders: green chile and cheddar, provolone and mushroom, bacon and blue cheese.*

They quickly dispatch this surfeit of munchies, and they follow-up with a second course: a shared order of chile nachos, washed down by another round of beer.

"This is the best meal I've had all trip," says Lathom, licking his fingers when the nachos are gone. "Maybe the whole year. Epicurean."

"I've been thinking about the story idea you laid on me," says Blythe. "I like it. I even did some research on my phone at the bookstore. Turns out, travel guides are a relatively new phenomenon, so when it comes to vintage, it really means travel *brochures* that fold out like an accordion. They were produced as giveaways by banks or oil companies or local chambers of commerce."

"1933," says Lathom.

"Huh?"

"That's the year your protagonist should find himself in your time-travel story. Whatever travel guide or brochure you choose, it should be from 1933. And make it December—maybe a Christmas story."

"Why?"

"Because there aren't enough Christmas stories anymore."

"I mean, why 1933?"

"December 1933 is when Prohibition ended," says Lathom. "Must have been one helluva Christmas and New Year's Eve." He winks. "Makes for good storytelling. All you need to figure out next is *where*."

"Any ideas about that?"

"You want me to do all your work for you? My advice is, let serendipity be your guide. Like I said before, find a real travel guide or brochure. Buy it, go there, live it—and then write it all up. But first read the vocabulary manual I just gave you."

"Jeez, what did I do with it?" Blythe looks around, can't see it anywhere, then checks the pocket of his leather jacket, which he'd draped around the stool. "Ah, here it is."

A pretty middle-aged woman stands smiling in front of Lathom.

"I'm sorry," he says, befuddled by her attention. "Do I know you?"

"I was at your book signing just now," she says.

"The one without books?" Lathom laughs sourly.

"Uh-huh. I enjoyed your speech."

"But I didn't give one."

"Okay, then I liked how you answered questions." She puts her hand on his wrist briefly. "I thought it was cute. May I buy you a drink?"

Lathom glances at Blythe, then back at the woman, and shrugs. "Why not?"

Her name is Theodora. She looks to be in her late-forties,

rounded in the right places, with intense brown eyes, blonde hair and brown roots. And she continues her touchy-feely flirtation with Lathom.

"So, what do you do, Theodora?" asks Lathom.

"I'm a poo provider."

"You're a *what?*" The author is unsure he has heard properly, mindful that he is somewhat stoned.

"I donate my poo." She pauses. "For pay, of course."

"Of course." Lathom chuckles. "How does *that* work?"

"I naturally produce what's known as super stools."

"Super *what?*" Lathom remains amused—and bewildered.

"Super poo—as in turds."

"Yeah, I get that." He nods. "I think." He shakes his head. "But I still don't understand exactly what you're talking about."

"It's like this," says Theodora, smiling. "My poo teems with good bacteria. I'm what they call a *super-donor*. Hospitals give my poo to patients with gut problems—things like inflammatory bowel disease or colitis. It's very important because your gut is your second brain. The bacteria in your gut is neuro-active. That's how the phrase *gut instinct* got born."

"But... how?"

"Fecal transplantation."

"What?"

"My super-stools are delivered directly to the colons of patients in need through a colonoscope."

Lathom remains incredulous. "But what makes *your* stool so special?"

Theodora shrugs. "For a start, I'm vegan. But there's much more to it than that. My only particular microbiome produces super-poo because I haven't taken antibiotics for many years. Antibiotics kill good bacteria. In fact, it's people who've had too many antibiotics in their lives that are most in need of my poo."

"And that's your job?"

"Uh-huh." She nods earnestly. "For every sixty grams of my super-poo I earn forty dollars. Which means, with the right amount of fiber I can bring in six hundred dollars a week." She pauses, smiling with pride. "And with fecal grafting growing ever more popular, my poo is in more demand than ever."

Lathom doesn't know whether to shake or nod his head, so he ends up doing both. "Fecal grafting?"

"It's when your whole colony of bowel bacteria is replaced by another. When gut patients do this, all kinds of bad health issues get improved."

As the effects of the cannabis from the cookies intensify, Lathom begins to question whether or not he's being conned by this odd woman; worse, Blythe is nowhere to be seen and his disappearance causes a wave of paranoia to wash over the author's thinking process.

Lathom's fear compounds exponentially when Theodora invites him back to her place nearby for a nightcap, causing his brain to fill with images of James Caan tied to a bed in a woodsy cabin in the wilds of somewhere—*was it Oregon?*

And then Theodora even starts to look like Annie

Wilkes—the psychopathic fan played by Kathy Bates in the movie *Misery*.

"Excuse me," says Lathom, feeling desperate now. "Need to use the john."

En route, he searches the bar—and the restroom—for Blythe, to no avail.

"I've settled your tab," Theodora says upon Lathom's return. "Shall we go now?"

Her words resonate around Lathom's mind in a slow-motion phantasmagoria of color and voices.

"No, no, no, no, no." Lathom waves her off, eyes full of fear. "I need to call a taxi."

"Where are you going?"

"My hotel."

"I'll take you."

"No, no, no, no, no. I just need a cab." He turns. "Bartender, can you call me a taxi?"

"Everything's Uber around here—don't you use Uber?"

"Can you call one for me?"

"It'll get charged to my card."

"I'll pay you the cash plus a few bucks extra."

"Where are you going?"

Lathom looks at Kathy Bates or Annie Wilkes, or whoever the hell she is, shields his mouth away from her. "The Heathman," he whispers.

His perceived kidnapper overhears. "Not far," she says. "C'mon I'll drive you myself."

And then Jasmine pops up from out of nowhere.

Lathom isn't sure it's really her, that maybe he's hallu-cinating.

"Are you all right?" she asks, studying his glazed eyes.

"No, I'm not all right," he half whispers, half hisses, shaking his head. "I'm definitely not all right. Where's Blythe?"

"Don't know." Jasmine glances up and down the bar and around. "I just got here, haven't seen him."

"Can you get me out of here?" Lathom implores. "I can't think straight and my mind is playing games with me. I need to get back to my room where it's safe."

"You want me you call you an Uber?" Jasmine consults her phone and taps a key. "There are three within a couple blocks."

"Please come with me," Lathom practically begs. "See me to the elevator in the lobby. I'll pay both ways so you can come straight back here."

"Uber is already here—let's go."

31.

Around nine a.m., Blythe knocks on the door of Lathom's hotel room.

No answer.

"Not again," he mumbles to himself.

He's boogied to PDX for a flight home. And if he's already checked through security into the departure lounge, I won't be able to get through to fetch him.

Blythe shakes his head in self-disgust for not being more vigilant with his charge. And now, feeling sorry for himself, and lamenting the job he was sure to lose—as certain as losing his author—Blythe wanders through a light drizzle to Pioneer Square, into Portland's very first Starbucks, to contemplate his plight over an Americano while vacantly looking through plate glass at the old courthouse on the other side of the square.

Options, options.

There aren't many.

In fact, only one: Drive back to LA.

Alone.

The overcast sky does not improve Blythe's mood as he trudges back to The Heathman.

Thinking he might as well fill his stomach before hitting the road, Blythe wanders into Headwaters to scope out their breakfast menu… and—lo and behold—there he is, the novelist, wearing his signature straw fedora, sitting by himself at a table for two by a window overlooking Broadway, his back to the world, a favored pose, sipping black coffee.

Blythe walks around him and touches the chair opposite. "May I?"

Lathom looks up. "You!"

Blythe tilts his head. "I *think* it's me."

"Then you're doing better than me," snaps Lathom. "I wasn't sure *who* I was when I woke up this morning. What the dickens happened to you last night? You abandoned me—full knowing I was out of my mind on pot!"

Blythe plops down. "You seemed like you were having a good time." He winks. "Two's company, three's a crowd, no?"

"And you say *I* talk in clichés?" Lathom throws up his arms. "There was a reason for that woman's blandishment."

"Huh-what?"

"Look it up! She was going to kidnap and torture me! No thanks to you, I might add."

"Kidnap and torture you? What makes you think that?"

"Wasn't it obvious?"

Blythe shrugs. "Not to me."

"Have you not seen the movie *Misery?* A deranged fan trying to lure a famous writer back to her place so she can torture him to death? That's what was going down last night."

"I hardly think…"

"What *were* you thinking, leaving me stoned out of my mind on pot? You're supposed to be my *escort* for chrissakes!"

"She seemed perfectly nice and she really liked you."

"Well, she looked like Kathy Bates to me." Lathom shivers. "Were you there when she talked about what she does for a living—or had you already absconded?"

Blythe shakes his head. "I don't recall."

"Never mind." Lathom turns to look over his shoulder for Kathy Bates. "It is filthy damp in this town and I think I caught a cold, and now it's going to my ear. Always happens when I travel, goes straight to my ear, all the germs everyone is happy to spread and of course my Purell is never around when I need it. Once the germs get into my system, never fails, they always bunch together and make a beeline for my left ear."

A server stops to refill Lathom's coffee cup and to offer some java to Blythe.

"No thanks, just had some." He turns to Lathom as the server disappears. "So, I guess you'll be catching a flight home?" He asks this because he is already resigned to this development and thus cannot be bothered to deliver the spiel he'd planned about how this was exactly what the wicked Francine Fassbender wanted and that it would undoubtedly play right into her hands for legally stopping the advance due him, rendering Lathom wholly dependent on royalties many months ahead—though, the way things were going, royalties now seemed like pie in the sky.

Lathom shakes his head. "You crazy? I can't fly with an earache coming on—it would blow my eardrum out. And I lost my brand-new scarf, probably left it at that damn bar."

"Then we might as well drive to Seattle," says Blythe, brightening. "It's only three hours away. That way, you'll get your hotel bill covered by the publisher and you can catch a nonstop flight home from Seattle when you're better."

Lathom shrugs. "Why not? Things can hardly get much worse than they already are, can they?"

32.

"IT's damp and dark, and I caught a bug and it's turning into an earache."

"Sorry to hear. Have you seen today's New York Times?"

"No, why?"

Silence on the other end.

"Out with it!" snaps Lathom.

"They did a story on you today."

"Today? Why today? Today's not Sunday. I should be in the Sunday Book section, no?"

"Yes, you should. But you're not. Because this isn't about your book."

"Not about my book?"

"No. You're in the *legal* section."

"The *what?* Why?"

"They ran a story about a lawsuit filed against you in Federal Court for copyright infringement."

"Why would the New York Times care about that!" thunders Lathom. "I was just served a few days ago, for chrissakes! And why are they so interested in a shake-down—which is what this is—instead of the publication of my first novel in thirty years?" He pauses to assess what's going on. "IS SOMEBODY TRYING TO SABOTAGE ME?"

"No point yelling at me," says Downey. "I'm on *your* side. I spoke with your editor at Mulberry. They're not happy about this story either."

"Then why don't they do something about it?"

"They are. They're thinking of cancelling the rest of your book tour."

"Well, that's the best damn news I've heard all week! Does that mean I can go home now?"

"No, no, no. Don't do anything like that. Stick to the tour. They haven't made a decision."

"Aside from anything else, isn't a man presumed innocent until found guilty by a jury of his peers? Isn't the onus on the plaintiff, a scam artist in this case, to prove his *allegations* with actual *evidence?*"

"You'd have to ask your lawyer about that."

And that's exactly what Lathom does. His next call is to Glenn Pioche.

Who does not pick up.

Lathom curses and leaves a terse message to call him back.

And then it's time to check out.

33.

WITHIN a few minutes of hitting the road, Blythe and Lathom are rolling across the Portland-Vancouver Interstate Bridge into Washington State.

"This is where I should move to," says Lathom, perking to the exit ramp signage.

"Why's that?" asks Blythe.

"I've read about Vancouver. Best deal in the country."

"How so?"

"No sales tax in Oregon, no state income tax in Washington.

"Live in Vancouver, cross the bridge for all your shopping needs in Portland. Beat the thieves."

Beyond the bridge, they pick up speed on The Grapevine when Lathom senses something—a presence, perhaps—missing from the car.

He turns, by reflex, to see what exactly is remiss.

Lathom is stunned by what he sees; rather, an *absence* of what he expected to see.

"Where the hell is Scallywag?"

Blythe swings his head 180-degrees from the road ahead just long enough to confirm that Scallywag's aquarium is no longer lodged upon the backseat, and Lathom's bearded dragon gone along with it.

"Somebody took Scallywag!" Lathom explodes.

"When did you last see it?" asks Blythe.

"Scallywag is not an *it*. Never mind when *I* last saw Scallywag, which was just before going into that cockama-mie pot-shop-of-a-new-age-hippie-bookstore last night. You're the one who's been driving this vehicle. When did *you* last see him?"

Blythe shrugs. "I can't say, I don't know."

"I can't say, I don't know," Lathom mimics. "Think! Where else did you go last night?"

"I walked around, grabbed a beer in some bar and drove back to the hotel. That's it."

"So, you're saying you don't know if Scallywag was kidnapped where we parked near the bookstore or back at the hotel?"

Blythe shrugs.

"Did you valet the car?"

"Of course, expenses."

"You think the valet stole Scallywag?"

"I don't know why *anyone* would steal a bearded dragon," says Blythe. "Maybe as a joke?"

"As a joke? I don't see anything remotely funny about kidnapping a bearded dragon!"

"No, I didn't mean it like that."

"Then what do you mean?" Lathom wails. "Never mind, it doesn't matter what you think. I can't believe my little Scallywag is gone, just like that. We've been together over five years. He was my best friend in the whole world—my *only* friend."

Blythe senses Lathom's genuine anguish. "Want me to turn around, go back to Portland and look for him?"

"Where? How? Gone is gone!"

Blythe scratches his head, at a loss for words.

Lathom turns inward and quiet, as a life without his beloved, if inert, bearded dragon sinks in.

"Goddam book tour," he finally mutters. "I'm never writing another book. No, I take that back. I'll write—but I'll never publish again. Ever. And if I ever do…" Lathom pounds his right fist into his left hand, "…I'm dedicating what I write to poor Scallywag." He retreats into the recesses of his mind, then re-erupts. "It was probably one of those ladies at the book signing! They wanted a piece of me, couldn't get it, so they took Scallywag instead. Maybe it was Kathy Bates! Poor Scallywag—he's going to be tortured to death in my place!"

"I don't think…"

"That's exactly right! You don't think. You weren't thinking straight last night, you got us both stoned on pot and then you lost Scally…!"

Lathom's tirade is interrupted by the whistling of his phone.

Glenn Pioche.

Lathom pounds the green button with his forefinger and answers with a mouthful in one breath: "In today's New York Times there is an article about the lawsuit against me, how the hell could that happen?"

"Easy," says Pioche. "This plaintiff is playing hardball. They're doing anything and everything they can to rattle your cage and prod you into settling with them. And that includes going to the media to embarrass you. They know the drill. Clearly, they've used these tactics many times against high-profile targets. I had my paralegal conduct a nationwide court record search and discovered our plaintiff is quite the vexatious litigant. It means he sues a lot."

"I know what *vexatious* means. I'm a writer."

"For this scumbag of a plaintiff, contacting media to drum up attention is business-as-usual. I spoke with the lawyer of one of his victims and uncovered his modus operandi. Turns out this guy doesn't even earn a living through photography."

"Then what...?"

"Oh, he postures himself as a high-quality photographer. He gets to know people and offers to photograph them as a gift. He gives them copies of the pictures and immediately registers copyright ownership with the U.S. Copyright Office. Then he waits and watches. He trolls the Internet to see if any of the photos he gave away for free have been used on social media. When one turns up—maybe because somebody put it on Facebook or Instagram—he threatens a lawsuit unless they pay him $1500 for the photoshoot that was supposed to be a gift." He pauses. "The people he threatens usually settle. No one wants to be sued and have to retain a lawyer."

"Yes, I can appreciate that firsthand," says Lathom.

"So, they pay him to go away. If they don't pay, he files a lawsuit using a scummy contingency lawyer who's in it for an easy third of any money collected. They turn the screws with multiple motions and depositions—and whatever media exposure they can muster—until the defendant can't take it anymore and caves."

"And he gets away with this?"

"We estimate that for every person he's sued, ten probably settled to avoid a lawsuit before it was filed. He's probably pulling in a hundred grand a year from this scam—and never visits a darkroom."

"Except the one in his mind."

"Exactly."

Lathom disconnects the attorney as the pain in his rear-end and down his right leg begins to conspire with the pain growing in his left ear to create a full-on, all-out body ache.

"I hate doctors, but I need a one," he says to Blythe. "And I need Scallywag back. Why did I ever leave my home for this abominable book tour?"

"The mudslide?" Blythe offers with a side-glance.

"Yeah, right. I should have stuck with mud. At least I'd still have Scallywag."

Francine has the misfortune of calling Blythe this very moment to inquire about how things had gone in Portland.

"It's not going well," whispers Blythe, trying to snuggle the phone between his left ear and shoulder so he can talk hands-free.

"Is our *au-thor*," she enunciates *author* with obvious derision, "still causing trouble everywhere he stumbles?"

"No, he's good," says Blythe, glancing at Lathom. "But somebody stole his bearded dragon."

"His what?"

"It's a kind of lizard, his pet. It was in the backseat in an aquarium and now it's not."

"Serves him right," snaps Francine. "Who does he think he is bringing a lizard on a book tour with him?"

She does not realize that Lathom can hear her through the phone's earpiece. She also does not realize that Mulberry's author has just about had it.

With everything.

Especially this book tour.

But most especially *her.*

"Fuck you, bitch-witch!" he bellows.

Francine goes silent.

And then a siren sounds behind them.

Checking out his rearview mirror, Blythe realizes the red-and-blue lights are flashing for him; he's being pulled over.

"Can't talk while I'm driving," he says to a shocked Francine. "I'll call you back later."

"Ramp off at the next exit!" the cop booms through a bullhorn.

Blythe complies, slowing to a halt.

The State Patrol officer pulls up from behind, saunters over and bends down to speak through the driver-side window. "Do you know why I stopped you?"

Blythe shrugs. "Not really."

"Hands-free," he growls, "does not mean balancing a cell phone with your neck."

"I'm sorry, officer—it was my boss."

"Uh-huh. License and registration."

Blythe pulls out his wallet, from which he plucks his driver's license and hands it to the lawman before reaching into the glove compartment for the vehicle's rental agreement.

The officer looks at the license, leans down and squints to study Blythe's likeness compared with the photo.

"Blythe Lathom?"

Blythe's face flushes. "Yes, sir."

The police officer returns to his vehicle with the documents to run traces, check for warrants.

Lathom studies Blythe, who continues to stare straight ahead. "Why," he asks slowly, "did he say Blythe *Lathom?*"

Blythe shrugs, blushing—and seemingly lost for words.

The cop returns. "I'm going to let you off with a warning this time. *Don't* talk on your cellphone when you're driving."

"Thank you, officer—I truly appreciate that."

Blythe ignites the car, crosses the road ahead and ramps back onto the interstate.

"I still don't get it," says Lathom. "He looked at your driver's license and he said Blythe *Lathom*. He didn't see *my* license—and I don't think he recognized me as a famous author. So, what's going on here?" He studies Blythe, who steadies his gaze upon the road ahead, albeit with the expression of a deer caught in headlights.

"Is your last name Lathom?"

Blythe swallows hard. He nods. His mouth is dry. "Yes, sir," he manages. "It is."

"But that's *my* last name."

"I guess you don't have a monopoly on it."

"What the hell do you mean by that?"

"It's really very simple," says Blythe, pausing to compose himself.

"I'm listening."

"I'm your grandson."

"But I don't have a grandson!"

"Yes, you do," says Blythe. "Me."

34.

It is a whole minute later.

Lathom remains silent, speechless and somewhat flabbergasted. Finally, he speaks. "Aragnorisis? You must be kidding me. I understand you're using *my* last name on your driver's license. But how does that equate to you being my grandson?"

"It's like this," says Blythe. "You got my grandmother pregnant, she had a son—yours—and I was born a couple decades later."

Lathom takes a few seconds to digest this. "So, what you're telling me that in the course of twenty minutes I've lost a bearded dragon and gained a fully-grown grandson?"

Blythe shrugs, smiles sheepishly. "That's about the size of it."

"Hmm. Okay."

Lathom seems lost in wonder. "Assuming for one moment—and just one moment—what you're saying is actually *true*, when were you planning to tell me?"

Blythe shakes his head. "I wasn't."

"But… but… you're *here*, driving me on a *book tour*," says Lathom. "That's no accident, is it?"

Blythe utters "No," through pursed lips.

Silence.

Lathom puts out his arms, palms-up. "Well, are you going to explain?"

Blythe nods. "Yes, okay, I will."

"I'm listening."

"I got this job because I wanted to get to know my grandfather, the famous novelist."

He turns to look his grandfather in the eye. "You."

Lathom shakes his head, still in shock over this unexpected and unbelievable development. "How did you manage that?"

"I knew you had a new book coming out. So, I looked into how best to get a job that would bring me into close proximity with you. Media escort was perfect."

He shrugs. "It just worked out."

Lathom looks puzzled. "Okay, okay. But I still don't get how that makes you my grandson. I don't *have* a family."

"Yes, you do. An ex-wife and a daughter, right?"

Lathom shakes his head, vigorously. "Oh, no, I don't. They're not my family anymore. I haven't seen either of them in years. The only family I have—*had*—is Scallywag. And now *he's* gone. And you're making my earache worse by telling me I have a son and grandson I never knew I had."

They drive in silence the rest of the way to the very heart of Emerald City, a boutique hotel adjacent to Pike Place called Inn on the Market.

Lathom's first order of business after checking in: consult the concierge about a house doctor, who is duly summoned.

In advance of his arrival, Lathom straggles across the road to Steelhead Diner for a short-term cure of his own: a large tequila at the bar.

And an opportunity to brood about the bombshell Blythe had laid on him.

It is, Lathom decides, a sick practical joke, in spite of whatever the hell name is on Blythe's driver's license.

35.

THE doctor arrives, diagnoses Lathom with an ear infection and provides Amoxicillin from his bag.

Lathom swallows the first dose on the spot.

"I need to get home," he says. "Is it okay to fly?"

The doc somberly shakes his head. "I'd wait till the antibiotics kick in, give them a few days to kill the infection."

"What about my back and leg pain?" asks Lathom.

"Sounds like sciatica," says the doc. "Unfortunately, I can't make that go away as easily as an earache. You will probably need a chiropractor or an osteopath. To get you through the pain for a few days I'll write a prescription for hydrocodone."

Lathom is a wee wobbly, if feeling no pain (courtesy of his other physician, Dr. Don Julio), when he arrives just before six p.m. at The Puget Sound Book Company with Blythe, whom he had not seen or spoken to since their dialogue following the police cell phone incident.

The prescribed opiate, having neutralized Lathom's various symptoms, leaves him feeling bouyant, even euphoric, not least because he has reached the furthermost destination of this wretched book tour.

All is going well—meet-and-greet, refreshments, Q&A—until near the end when, after the bookstore manager takes the podium to thank their guest author and cue the audience to a round of book purchasing, Lathom softly pats her bottom with the palm of his hand.

"What?" She turns on him like a panther. "What did you just do?"

Lathom shrugs, bewildered. "Uh, nothing, I..."

"You put your hand on my ass."

"No, no, no—it was just a harmless tap. My hand never settled on your ass."

"How dare you talk dirty and trivialize a sexual assault!"

Says the indignant author, "You used the word *ass*, before me, madam. I merely echoed your own choice of language. And I did not sexually assault you."

"No? What do you call putting your grubby paw on me?"

"Masochism?"

"What?" she sneers. "Typical old white guy," she says, shaking her head.

Lathom's eyes widen. "Typical old white guy? Typical *dyke*, hates men."

That's when dialogue morphs into kerfuffle.

Unfortunately for Lathom, not only do several females in the audience side with the bookstore manager's version of events, but he himself owns up to an "innocuous" butt tap, which he justifies as endearment, not flirtation, and certainly not a sexual assault.

Seattle's finest, as progressive as they come, do not share Lathom's perspective or definitions, and once statements by all parties are duly noted, and a sergeant consulted, Christopher Lathom is read his rights, arrested for sexual assault and carted off to the pokey.

36.

At precisely eight o'clock the next morning, Christopher Lathom is escorted into a courtroom for arraignment, along with six other persons, mostly vagrants charged with petty crimes committed the night before.

Lathom takes his seat in the dock.

A taciturn (if slightly bored) judge works through the morning roster and, by 9:45, the disgraced and disheveled author is up to bat.

The judge, peering mournfully over reading specs at the alleged sexual deviant, quickly sets a date for a hearing and, as no bail is requested by the prosecution, releases the author on his own recognizance.

Blythe is waiting outside the police station when Lathom exits, having returned to reclaim his personal belongings, including his shoelaces lest he be tempted to hang himself—and tempted he most certainly was, partly due to humiliation, partly from lack of sleep, but mostly due to excruciating pain in his ear.

A photographer from the *Seattle Post-Intelligencer* is on hand to focus his lens on the bedraggled, unzipped and grim-faced author, whose mugshot—*sans* hat—had earlier exposed his bald pate and hoary countenance on a popular website called *The Smoking Gun.*

Lathom climbs into Blythe's car, snaps on his seatbelt, settles into his seat, closes his eyes briefly before turning to address his media escort. "I'm done."

"Don't blame you," says Blythe. "That was ridiculous. I'm done, too."

Lathom does not reply.

"I mean it," Blythe continues. "We're both done. Mulberry Press heard about what happened. They pulled the plug on the rest of your book tour." He pauses. "Not that it mattered, of course, since you were planning to fly home from here anyway."

Lathom opens his eyes and shakes his head. "Can't fly. Doctor's orders. And my earache is worse than ever. The damn cops refused to retrieve the medications from my room."

"Then I guess we're driving back."

"Not today." Lathom continues to shake his head, faster than before. "I'm somnolent."

"Huh?"

"Sleepy. Can't face a day on the road." He recloses his eyes. "I hardly slept all night, just laid wide awake on a cold hard bench." He shivers. "The worst part was the skanky stink. I've never been surrounded by so many germs. I need a bed. I need sleep."

"Bad news," says Blythe. "Our hotel reservation ended this morning. Plus, Mulberry's no longer paying. And even if you wanted to pay yourself, the inn says they're full to-night."

Lathom sighs, too tired to curse.

"I've already checked us out and put all your things in the trunk—I hope you don't mind."

"What a nightmare." Lathom reopens his eyes. "Any other hotels?"

"No. There's some kind of high tech convention going on and every hotel in the city is fully committed." He pauses. "I suggest we drive just a few hours, back to Portland, find a hotel there. Problem is, Mulberry ordered me to drive straight back to LA—nineteen hours. Can you believe that?"

Lathom looks at him in horror. "There's no way…"

"Figured as much. You can get a room in Portland, I'll sleep in the car."

Lathom adjusts his seat into a reclining position as far back as it will go and, within seconds, is sound asleep.

37.

Lᴀᴛʜᴏᴍ startles awake when the driving turns jerky from ramping off the interstate.

"Are we here already?" he asks.

"Stumptown," Blythe confirms.

"That went fast."

"You've been out solid. Any ideas for a hotel?"

"Let's stick with what we know."

But the Heathman has no rooms. Their desk crew recommends the Paramount Hotel, around the corner, where Blythe waits in the valet parking spot while Lathom saunters inside to scope it out, returning in a few minutes later to drop an envelope with key card onto Blythe's lap.

"Got you a room," says Lathom.

"But Mulberry's not paying and I can't afford…"

"I know. My treat. Thanks for sticking with me."

***

Inside his ninth-floor room overlooking the cityscape and Director Park below, Lathom rummages through his bag to find antibiotics, swallows one and crashes fully-clothed onto the comfortable king bed, appreciating—as never before—sheets, feather pillows and an eiderdown quilt.

38.

SOMETIME in the late afternoon, Lathom is stirred awake by the rumbling of his cell phone, which had been recharging on the bedside table after the battery went dead while in police custody.

He neither knows where he is nor how he got there as he picks up the phone and, totally flummoxed, vacantly answers.

"Where the hell are you?" asks Downey the literary agent.

"That's exactly what *I'd* like to know," says Lathom, not in jest but fully meaning it.

"You don't know where you are?"

Lathom looks around. "Not really. Maybe. I'm not sure." He gets up, ambles over to the window and gazes out at the city skyline. "I think I'm in Portland."

"You *think?*"

"I don't even know what time it is. What time is it?"

"For you, the eleventh hour," says Lathom. "Your little mishap or whatever it was in Seattle is all over the news. It even made it onto Drudge."

"Good for sales, maybe?"

"No. Bad for sales. Bad, period. What decade are you living in?"

"Not the thirties, forties or fifties, I gather," says Lathom coming to. "Can you imagine Hemingway getting busted for patting a woman's butt?"

"Hemingway died a long time ago and the world has changed since then. A lot."

"Yeah, well, maybe I need to go his way."

"Huh? What do you mean by that?"

"Sweet dreams, my valediction." Lathom drops his cell phone to the carpeted floor and examines the window frames. They are sliders. He applies pressure, pulling it forcefully to the left.

Bam!

The window frame smacks hard into a lock after opening a mere two inches.

Lathom shakes his head.

Nothing is going right on this book drive.

He trudges into the bathroom. And turns on both bathtub taps.

39.

THIS was Francine's response upon hearing from Blythe that he'd stopped to overnight in Portland with a badly beaten-down Lathom:

If you don't get that car back to LA by five p.m. tomorrow, you are toast, not only with Mulberry Press, but with the whole publishing industry, I'll see to it personally.

The other thing rattling Blythe is Lathom's almost total detachment, perhaps denial, of Blythe's fluky disclosure about their bloodline. Sure, he'd never intended to reveal their relation, and but for a random cop stop it would never have come up, but what the hell?

And thus, somewhat beaten himself, Blythe descends to the hotel's bar-and-grill, called Swine, adjacent to the lobby, and stools himself at the bar. He orders tequila, like his grandfather would, plus a beer to chase it.

The décor is wood and soft incandescent illuminations; Portland, with its ambient lighting, the king of cool.

Blythe is deep into his thoughts, as well as a second beer, when they are broken by a siren, first distant, then near, followed by the arrival of first responders in a shiny red rescue truck.

It takes a full minute, after the crew has already ascended to an upper floor, before Blythe equates their presence with Lathom's unstable frame of mind given the public humiliation his massive ego had just suffered.

He stiffens, fearing the worst.

40.

A few moments later, Lathom saunters into the bar, nods at Blythe and grabs the stool next to his.

"What's wrong?" he says to his former media escort. "You've lost your color."

"No, I'm okay." Blythe snaps out of his morbid thoughts. "How about you?"

Lathom shrugs. "A nap and a hot bath. I can tell you, sure beats a jail cell."

"Well, I've got news," says Blythe.

"Pray tell."

"I've been ordered back to LA. Which means I need to get up early and haul it sixteen hours. I'm guessing you're set to fly home from here, right?"

Lathom shrugs. "I don't know what I'm doing next. I don't even care."

The two men sip their potions in silence.

And suddenly a familiar figure prances in.

Jasmine is smiling broadly, her right hand covering something attached to her sweater.

Lathom looks over at her and can hardly believe his eyes.

"Scallywag!"

Jasmine nods joyfully.

"*You* took him?"

"Of course not." Jasmine mugs. "I *rescued* him. From the Oregon Humane Society."

"But... how...?"

"Blythe called around and discovered they had a bearded dragon in their care so I went to check it out—and there he was!"

Lathom gently loosens Scallywag from Jasmine's sweater and reattaches him to his safari vest, just below the neck.

"Did they tell you how Scallywag got there?"

"All they would say is that someone thought he was being neglected in the car wherever it was parked. But it's possible someone took Scallywag and decided he was too much trouble to take care of—who knows? The truth is always in the moment and after that elusive. Are you guys still on target for Ashlantis?"

"Ass-land?" Lathom shakes his head. "I think not."

"The book tour was cancelled," adds Blythe.

"By whom?"

"The publisher, Mulberry Press. I've been ordered to drive all the way back to LA tomorrow."

"Aunt Francine? I'll talk to her."

"Don't talk to that bitch-witch on my account," Lathom lobs in. "I made a booking, I'm flying home from here tomorrow afternoon. By the way," he adds, "thanks for coming to my rescue the other night."

"How do you mean?"

"At that bar, after the book signing—getting me out of there."

Jasmine shakes her head, uncomprehending. "I still don't know what you mean."

"You're telling me you didn't call an Uber and see me back to my hotel?"

"I have no idea what you're talking about," says a doe-eyed Jasmine. "This is the first time I've seen you since we were at that awesome bookstore on Northwest 23rd Street."

Lathom ponders this. "I must have been higher than I thought. But if not you, who got me back safely?"

Jasmine giggles. "Maybe it was your guardian angel *posing* as me." She has a new thought. "May I hitch a ride with you two as far as San Francisco?"

41.

DINNER is at Swank, other side of the lobby; same ambience, full bar, but with a full dinner menu.

Jasmine had departed to prepare for the road trip ahead, so only Lathom and Blythe are stooled at the corner of the bar, better able to look at one another.

"I have a new idea for a story," says Lathom. "Assuming you still want to be a writer."

"Why would I not want that?"

"After seeing what I, a writer, has been through this trip?" He holds up both hands, palms out. "I know, I know—you want to be a writer because you think I'm your grandfather and you want to be like me."

"You *are* my grandfather."

"So you've said. But just because you say so, and your last name is Lathom, doesn't make it so."

"It's not the most common name."

"You could have changed it legally."

"Look, I understand you're a little paranoid, what with the whole scenario with Kathy Bates flirting with you, and germs conspiring to make you sick…"

"They did!"

"But I'm not looking for any money from you…"

"Well, it would be your hard luck if you were. I don't have any. The only thing I had of any value was my papers—and I already sold them to a university and spent all the money supporting myself while taking decades to write a damn novel nobody seems to care about." Lathom pauses. "But do humor me. How is it I'm supposedly your grandfather?"

"You remember talking about how happy you were on a houseboat in Sausalito with a woman that was the love of your life?"

"Did I?"

Blythe nods. "You did, during our first leg on the ride north." He pauses. "That woman was my grandmother."

Lathom nods uncertainly. "That's easy. As you say, I already talked about it."

"Her name was Wendy."

Lathom flinches, jolted by this revelation.

"And you didn't tell me *that*," Blythe continues. "My Grandma Wendy had long red hair and green eyes. You didn't talk about that, either."

"You said *had*." Lathom stiffens. "Where is she?"

"Uh, she's not around."

Lathom's expression is pained. "Not around?"

"Gone. She had a son. *Your* son, *my* father." Blythe breathes heavily. "He got married and had me."

He pauses again. "And when I was six, my dad got sent to Afghanistan as a Green Beret. And..."

Blythe chokes up, "he was killed in a firefight."

Both men sit in silence.

"And your mother?" Lathom finally asks.

"A whole other story," he says. "Suffice to say, I was raised by my Grandma Wendy."

Lathom takes his own deep breath and sighs. "So, you're telling me I had a son who was dumb enough to enlist in the army and get himself killed in an ill-conceived war?"

"That's how you label your own son?" Blythe snaps. "Dumb?" He regains his composure and lowers his voice.

"My father, your son," he softly explains, "was already in the army before the war started. He signed up for the educational opportunities they offered." He pauses. "Money was always an issue for him and his mom without a dad around. Why else do you think we ended up in Blythe? And when he was deployed for active duty abroad, he went willingly. I'm proud of my dad. And I'm sorry if you're not."

Lathom remains silent, digesting this.

"It wasn't easy for my grandmother to have her only son killed. Or me, losing my dad. We were a tight unit, the three of us. It broke both our hearts in so many pieces..." Blythe goes silent, chin aquiver. "On a lighter note," he continues, "I always wanted to be a writer ever since

I could remember. While other kids in first grade would say *fireman* and *policeman* when asked what they wanted to be when they grew up, I'd say *writer*. And when my grandmother finally told me who my grandfather was... is... I finally knew why."

For the first time since being confronted with this news, Lathom comprehends that Blythe is genuinely his grandson, leaving him somewhat shaken and stirred, partly because the love of his life, Wendy, who he always believed he might one day reconnect with, was *gone*. Gone forever. And partly because the young man sitting next to him was truly his flesh and blood.

"You're lucky," Lathom finally says, avoiding eye contact.

"How's that?"

"I would've been a lousy grandfather. You were better off without me in your life. You had a fine grandmother. Why would you want to ruin that?"

"I don't. My grandmother is great. Uh, was great. I just wanted to know you better, know my granddad, without my granddad ever knowing it. Sorry it didn't work out that way."

Lathom turns to his grandson. "What do you expect me to do with this?"

"Nothing," says Blythe, returning his gaze.

"Take a DNA test?"

Blythe shakes his head sadly. "No reason for that. I know it's true. And like I said, I'm not looking for anything."

"You tell me I have a grandson I never knew about and you're it and I'm supposed to simply forget about it?"

Blythe sighs. "It doesn't matter to me. That's not why I'm here."

"Then why are you here?"

"I already told you. I wanted to see you, up close. Experience you. Better understand who I am, where I came from."

"So, did you get what you came for?"

Blythe takes a few long moments to consider the question. "Working on it."

"Okay, so while you're working on it, may I tell you the new story idea I dreamt up for you? Literally. Because it's based on a dream I had while in a deep sleep this afternoon."

"You get all your ideas from dreams?" asks Blythe, mildly disgusted by the change of subject. "Never mind, go for it."

"The main character is a judge."

"As in a court of law?"

Lathom nods. "Probably brought on by my judicial experience this morning."

"No doubt."

"I'd title it The Hottest Ticket in Town. This particular judge is a buffoon—but a very entertaining buffoon. He's so entertaining that the public line up to get into his courtroom every morning just to be entertained by his outrageous antics. As eccentric as he is, he has absolute authority over everyone inside his courtroom—and no one has the authority to object or oust him from his job.

"He cusses at everyone, burps and farts incessantly, and throws objects at prosecution and defense attorneys when they annoy him. He insults the marshals mercilessly and they still have to protect him. He especially has fun with jurors, especially those who try to escape jury duty with various excuses.

"Then one day, a juror announces that he is a proponent of Jury Nullification of Law..."

"Jury *what?*"

"Jury Power." Lathom feeds lettuce from the salad he ordered to Scallywag, who continues to cling to his sweater, unwilling to let go after his animal shelter ordeal. "It's when a juror ignores the judge's evidentiary instructions and puts the *law* on trial. In other words, this juror will vote to acquit even if the evidence says the defendant is guilty on the basis that the juror thinks the law that got broken was a dumb law. It becomes a power struggle between the temperamental judge and the stoic juror and, ultimately, the *hottest ticket in town.*"

Blythe is silent a long while.

"You don't like it?" asks Lathom.

Blythe shrugs. "I've got my mind on other things."

"Yeah, I get that."

"Get what?"

"If I were your age, I'd have fallen in love with Jasmine by now. That's what happens when you put boys and girls together."

"Not my type."

Lathom sighs. "I can't imagine why not."

"In that case I'll explain why." Blythe looks away, composes himself and looks back. "I'm gay."

Lathom takes a long time to consider this, unsure whether Blythe is pulling his leg or not. "Gay? Really?"

"Truly."

"How can a grandson of mine be *gay?*"

"So, I guess you finally accept I'm your grandson. But you can't accept that I'm gay?"

Lathom shrugs, non-committal; in fact, he's rather speechless.

"Really? Nothing?"

"I don't know what you want from me."

"I told you, I don't want anything. Well, maybe a few writing tips—but I already got that on the drive up."

"So, what's left?"

Blythe shakes his head. "You're right." He slides off his bar stool and ambles off. "Have a nice flight home."

"Are you walking out on me?" calls Lathom.

Blythe turns on the threshold between Swank and the lobby. "You mean like you did to me?"

"But I never knew you existed."

"I meant in Ashland, the bus station—remember?"

"Oh."

"See ya."

PART FOUR

42.

LATHOM is completely worn out from his brush with feminism, law enforcement and the judicial system, and maybe a little wobbly from drink and hydrocodone, when, after draining his third tequila, he ambles out into Portland's moist night for fresh air and a walk.

This is not something he would normally do. But the author is feeling far from normal as he strolls to the other side of Director Park and, crossing Yamhill Street, carelessly steps into the path of an oncoming trolley.

He turns and freezes. And finds himself staring death in the face.

The trolley's brakes are useless in such close proximity.

The only thing between life and death for Lathom is the quick thinking of a homeless man, one of many such persons that populate downtown; a homeless man who jumps into action and, seconds before impact, pulls Lathom from harm's way, thus saving his life.

Trembling, rather shocked and feeling deep gratitude for his unlikely savior, Lathom pulls out his wallet (from a back pocket, sciatic nerve be damned). He plucks out a ten-dollar bill and hands it to the scruffy, bearded young man who, in appreciation of the handout, hugs the man he just saved.

Already dog-tired, Lathom's near-death experience leaves him totally drained and so he circles back to his hotel for the deepest, longest and perhaps sweetest sleep of his life.

43.

BLYTHE and Jasmine are rolling in light traffic halfway between Portland and Salem when Blythe's smartphone jingles. He recognizes Lathom's number and is sorely tempted not to answer, but gives in and places the call on speaker so he can drive hands-free and not risk any further attention from Oregon's state troopers.

"I lost my wallet," Lathom blurts.

"I'm fine, thanks, how are you?" says Blythe.

"I just told you, I lost my wallet, which means I'm not at all good."

"Sorry to hear."

"I think my pocket got picked last night by a homeless guy. I can't get on a plane without ID and my driver's license was in my wallet."

"I get your situation," says Blythe. "But what exactly does that have to do with *me*?

"You're my driver."

"Past tense, Mister Lathom. I *was* your driver. The book tour is over. It got terminated—remember? Which means, my job driving you also got terminated. In fact, my instructions are, quite specifically, *not* to drive you."

"That's harsh."

"Maybe take a bus?"

"My credit cards and cash are gone, too," says Lathom. "I'm stuck here with Scallywag, who had to sleep in the bathtub last night."

"What am I supposed to do about that?"

"Take me with you?"

Somewhat exasperated, Blythe says, "We're already on the road. If I turn back now, I won't make it to LA on time and I'll get fired."

"But I'm your grandfather," says Lathom.

"What?" Blythe is not sure whether to be honored by this admission—or laugh at the incongruity. "You dare use that *against* me?"

"You can't just leave your grandfather stranded in a strange—*really* strange—city, without money and ID after driving me all the way up here."

Blythe looks to Jasmine, who returns his gaze with her naturally empathetic eyes, albeit a size larger than usual.

"You think," he says to Jasmine, "you can talk to your Aunt Francine and maybe buy me some time?"

"You think," says Jasmine, "you can explain what he means by saying he's your grandfather?"

44.

"You know the old adage," mutters Lathom, climbing into the backseat with one hand holding Scallywag in place on his vest and the other steadying his balance. "Let no good deed go unpunished."

"So, you're saying *I'll* be punished for turning around and driving all the way back for you?" asks Blythe.

"No, no." Lathom settles in. "I'm referring to *me.*"

"But of course," sighs Blythe.

"Me-me-me!" sings Jasmine in operatic voice.

"I give a guy ten bucks and he steals my wallet. How could I be so stupid, letting him hug me?"

"You probably *needed* a hug." Blythe laughs sourly. "I'm guessing the last time somebody hugged you was decades ago."

"Smartass," says Lathom.

"I don't have to be professionally polite anymore," says

Blythe. "Consider yourself lucky we returned to save your ass."

Jasmine perks up. "I understand you two are related?"

"Secret's out," says Blythe to Lathom. "She overheard our phone conversation."

"I told you she was a spy."

Blythe turns to Jasmine. "I'd be grateful if you don't happen to mention it to your aunt."

"She doesn't know?"

"No one was supposed to know, not even *him*." Blythe motions with a backhand wave. "He didn't know until finding out by accident a couple days ago—an incident also involving a cell phone."

"This is so poetic," says Jasmine.

"Really?" Blythe shrugs. "Why am I not feeling it?"

Jasmine turns to face Lathom in the backseat. "Are you not happy to meet a grandson you never knew you had?"

"I already have a daughter who refuses to talk to me," says Lathom.

"What is that supposed to mean?"

"Simple." Lathom folds his arms. "It means I'm a failure as a father. There's no point in me trying to pretend I can ever *not* be a failure as a father. Or *grand*father, by extension. Trust me, I'm doing Blythe a huge favor by not making a big deal out of this." He pauses. "Blythe had a wonderful grandmother. He got along just fine without me till now. You know the old adage, if it ain't broke don't fix it."

Blythe rolls his eyes, somewhat disgusted by Lathom's

trivializing of a matter so very near and dear to him. "Another cliché? Unbelievable. To think I sought writing advice from you."

Jasmine accesses her smart phone and taps out a number.

"Yes, everything's fine," she says to Aunt Francine. "I'm on the road with Blythe on schedule." She pauses. "I have a huge favor to ask."

She lowers her voice to barely a whisper.

45.

"Okay, here's the deal," says Jasmine, addressing her fellow road warriors as the road continues to unwind before them. "You, Blythe, do not have to drive all the way to LA today. I told my aunt I'd like to stay near Mount Shasta overnight to double-check the monastery, and she said okay."

Blythe heaves a sigh of relief. "Works for me—and they're still paying for my hotel?"

"Yes, she says you're still on the payroll, with expenses."

"Is Mulberry paying for *your* little vacation?" Lathom asks Jasmine.

"I'm doing this for *you,* mister," says Jasmine. "Dispel whatever negative thoughts you may have in your mind. My aunt doesn't know you're still with us."

"But why Shasta?" asks Lathom. "We already did that."

"We didn't stay overnight, and now we can. And it makes sense because it's halfway to San Francisco, where I'm headed. Plus, we didn't have enough time on our way up to enjoy the mountain's magical power."

"Ah, forgive me," says Lathom, a tad sarcastic. "I forgot about the magic."

"You're forgiven. We should stop in Ashlantis for something to eat," she adds, "I'm out of Lithia water and need a refill for taking some home with me." She winks and displays a wicked grin. "Maybe I'll even give some to Aunt Francine."

46.

BLYTHE pulls into a parking space on East Main Street in the heart of Ashland and all three alight onto the pavement.

Passing a bookstore, something in that shop's window catches Jasmine's eye.

"Look," she points.

"A poster in the window with our esteemed author's picture on it."

Blythe stops in his tracks to look up at the store's signage.

Bloomsbury Books.

From his back pocket, he plucks the typed itinerary and studies it closely.

"This is the bookstore," he says to Lathom, "where you were supposed to have an event... *tonight!*"

"There's a huge crowd in there," says Jasmine, somewhat excited.

"And look—isn't that your book—*lots* of your books—in the window? *Day of the Rabbits?*"

"Yes." Lathom shrugs. "But why should it matter? Mulberry cancelled the tour. Their problem, not mine. Finito bon soir."

"I'm going in," says Jasmine.

"I'll be at the bar in that hotel we stayed at," says Lathom, wandering off. "I see it up ahead."

Blythe can't make up his mind whom to follow, so he stands in place, shuffling, curious to hear whatever intel Jasmine turns up.

47.

It occurs to Lathom, sitting upon a stool inside Lark, that he has not experienced any shooting pains in his leg all day. And, thanks to the amoxicillin cutting in, the ache in his ear seems also to have dissipated. He orders a beer, instead of tequila, to quench his thirst.

"Do you want to run a tab?" asks the bartender.

Realizing he has no wallet and thus no way to make payment, Lathom nods.

He is halfway into his beer, considering his options for a second drink, when Jasmine bursts into the art deco watering hole, *Just Blythe* two steps behind her.

She erupts breathlessly. "Nobody told them the event was cancelled! There are over fifty people inside waiting to see you and buy signed books!"

"So what?" Lathom raises his glass, takes a sip. "I don't have to do that anymore because the tour's off." He studies their awed faces. "Look, you two, I hate doing this stuff—plus it only gets me into trouble. Let's just order some food and keep rolling, let Mulberry be embarrassed by their screw-up."

Jasmine shakes her head. "You need to do this. For yourself, not Mulberry. Or to spite Mulberry. Do this because *you* want to."

"But I *don't* want to."

"Please, Mister Lathom, for once just allow your ego to *amuse* you, not *abuse* you. And never mind your publisher, or my aunt. You're going to do this for *you*, no one else. Drink up, we're going, right now, even if I have to drag you there myself."

When Lathom enters Bloomsbury Books he is met with a rousing welcome of applause from approximately five dozen persons in attendance.

His first inclination is to believe he is hallucinating because this unanticipated scenario otherwise makes no sense to him.

Might it be merely a figment of his imagination, as in cannabis flashback?

This event was supposed to have been cancelled. He was in Ass-land only because he'd had his wallet filched and needed to travel by road and stopped in (at this precise time, by chance) for quick refreshment before continuing on, tail between his legs, to points south.

And so, it is a bewildered, surprised and even somewhat humbled author who joins the female bookstore manager at the lectern, this time very conscientiously keeping his hands to himself.

"We are fortunate to have with us this evening one of this country's most acclaimed authors, the inimitable Christopher Lathom," she announces, evolving into a laudatory introduction of epic proportions, concluding with a brief narrative of Lathom's new novel, which, to his mind, could not have been articulated so eloquently without her having actually read it.

And then she turns the lectern over to Lathom, prompting another round of wild applause.

"I am truly amazed to be here," Lathom announces to the crowd, "for reasons not worth getting into. All I can say is, after what I've been through on this book tour, up and down the west coast, I am delighted to be here among you all. I have always believed that my writing speaks for itself and that an author's time is best spent writing rather than *talking* about writing. But your unexpected presence here—unexpected by me, for reasons, as I said, not worth going into—this evening has proven me wrong. And," he adds with a chuckle, "I'm *never* wrong."

As is Lathom's style, he opens the forum to Q&A and this time does a masterful job, full of verve, answering even the most trivial of questions with the same descriptive elegance reflected in his writing.

When asked, as he was in Healdsburg, who most influenced him as a writer, Lathom reflects thoughtfully.

"Gordon Lish, a longtime editor at Knopf and author of

novels himself, described the process as waving a magic wand. My pen is my magic wand and with it I create my own universe. Terry Southern advised writers to astonish. Henry Miller advocated joyousness. And Tom Robbins, along with Douglas Adams, are high on whimsy and irony. I'd like to think all of these elements are incorporated in my writing."

While most other questions deal with his writing habits and why he took so long to publish a second novel, one woman asks about his arraignment in Seattle.

Rather than taking offense, Lathom shrugs and says, "I still don't know what I did wrong other than not pay attention to progressive trends, which I suppose can happen when you lead a solitary life as a writer, hidden away, as I choose to be, from the world and so-called civilization in general. Maybe part of me is trapped by the romance of Hemingway's time. If I'm out in public, which I prefer not to be, I'm prone to rumbustiousness." He raises his hands in mock surrender.

"Shoot me."

Nobody shoots. Only sympathetic smiles abound.

And then the inevitable question: why the book is titled *Day of the Rabbits*?

Lathom breathes deeply.

Blythe holds his own breath, with some apprehension, expecting the worst.

But Lathom does not become indignant and say *read the book*.

This is what comes out of his mouth:

"Day of the Rabbits is what the Club of Rome promulgated—in vain. Rabbits are a metaphor for reproduction, and in my novel, a metaphor for overpopulation. Our planet was once a healthy component of a cell—being our solar system—until it was infected by a destructive disease. Call it a cancer. And this disease is slowly suffocating, strangling, killing this component—Earth—and trying to spread to other organelles of the cell."

When all questions are asked and answered, every last one of them, Lathom sits behind a table fielding a queue of book-buyers, signing newly purchased copies of his novel while graciously allowing fans to pose with him for selfies, including Jasmine, who, although Lathom tries to waive the cost, insists on paying for a personalized, signed copy.

Watching from the sidelines, Blythe is utterly astounded by Lathom's panache handling of the crowd.

And proud of his grandpa.

48.

DRIVING across the border from Washington into Oregon, the clear night sky is illuminated by the shadowy brightness of a Full Beaver Moon; the rainclouds of Seattle and Portland, far behind them.

Jasmine has pinpointed McCloud, a small town on the south side of Mount Shasta, the ideal locus for them to rest their bones for the night—specifically, McCloud Mercantile Hotel. But first, in need of dinner, they park at Meat Market & Tavern, just in time for last food orders.

"I still can't believe how well you did at that bookstore," says Blythe, happy to be able to order a cold brew after driving all day.

Lathom shrugs, smiling. "It just didn't matter any-more."

"What didn't matter?"

"Any of it," he says. "Anything."

Jasmine smiles. "How's your sciatic nerve pain?"

"What pain?" Lathom grins and pats his back pocket. "No wallet."

"Funny how a thing like pain, and then no pain, can give a person a whole new perspective on life."

Jasmine winks. "And speaking of gratitude, what are your Thanksgiving plans?"

"Is that coming soon?" Lathom peers up from his menu.

Jasmine chuckles. "This coming Thursday."

Lathom shrugs. "Just another day for me. Vons stays open. And so does Starbucks."

"And you, Blythe?"

"No plans," he says softly, studying the menu.

"No family?" she prods.

Blythe steals a nervous glance at Lathom. "Not really. When my mother got pregnant with me, her parents wanted her to get an abortion, and when she wouldn't, they threw her out. Or she ran away, I don't know the whole story other than I got born and was brought up by my dad, and he never had another child—where will you be?" he adds, changing the subject.

"San Fran with my parents. As an omnist, I celebrate *all* holy days from around the world, but Thanksgiving is my favorite."

"Why?"

"Because it's not linked to any particular religion, and it's not about patriotism or war, just thankfulness—for *everyone* of all races and beliefs to celebrate."

"But you're vegetarian," says Lathom. "How can you celebrate Thanksgiving without turkey?"

Jasmine smiles. "The trimmings are *more* than a meal. And while everyone falls asleep on the sofa from tryptophan overdose I get to do the dishes and clean everything up."

"Doesn't sound like much of a holiday for you."

"Are you kidding? It's good therapy," says Jasmine. "It's the yin-yang of yoga."

"Huh?"

"Yoga is about *stillness*. Cleaning up is about *motion*. We, all human beings, are seventy percent water. Water needs motion to flow or it gets stagnant and cobwebby."

"Cobwebby," echoes Lathom. "How does someone get to know so much at your young age?"

"Maybe because every day, for me, is Thanksgiving," says Jasmine.

"How's that?" Lathom cups a hand over an ear.

"Why save gratitude for only one day of the year? *Every* day is a gift."

"Why have I never found that?"

"Maybe because you've never looked?" Jasmine lifts a pitcher and begins filling glasses. "And speaking of water, this..."

"No, no, no, no, no," says Lathom. "No Lithia-Sulphur cocktail for me."

Jasmine shakes her this head. "This is tap water from a seven-thousand-year-old aquiver beneath Mount Shasta—and quite probably the purest water in the world." She raises her glass. "A toast to gratitude—and naturally purified water."

"Not hungry?" says Lathom, pointing to her plate of vegetables, still half full.

"It's late," she says. "Food doesn't do you much good when you're sleeping. Plus, *hara hachi bu.*"

"Hair-what?" asks Blythe.

"It's Japanese," says Jasmine, "for never filling your stomach beyond eighty percent capacity."

49.

FEELING good about his book event in Ashland (at which he surprised himself), about his lower back and right leg not hurting and no earache either, Lathom emerges from the hotel all by himself at just past eleven o'clock at night to, as he might say, noctambulate.

The quiet submontane village of McCloud bathes in bright white light from the moon, casting numerous shadows, as Lathom wanders up Main Street, quiet and eerily still.

At West Colombero Drive he turns right, passes the Ax and Rose Public House (alas, too late for a nightcap) then, crossing California Street, finds himself standing directly in front of a charming log-cabin structure.

He walks a few steps nearer for a better look—*an historic one-room schoolhouse?*

No, a modest house of worship.

It had been a very long time since Lathom stepped foot

into a temple of any faith—probably the last time was a funeral, occasions he rarely attended, partly because, as a recluse, he did not stay in contact with many people and partly because he detested funerals, along with all non-secular pomp and ceremony.

Lathom had grown up without religion and when he gave spirituality any thought, which he rarely did—until the advent of Jasmine's perspective on life—he fell somewhere between atheism, agnosticism, and nihilism.

For whatever reason, maybe the full moon, maybe the moonlit mountain, which one could almost reach out and touch, Lathom walks up the wooden steps—eleven of them—to peer through one of two stained-glass windows built into double doors.

It is dark inside.

Out of nowhere, a small ball of light appears and races around the chapel before evanescing into the pine wall.

Intrigued, Lathom pushes on the door and, to his surprise, it creaks open.

He enters.

Moonlight streams through a large circular stained-glass window over this sanctuary's entrance, providing just enough illumination for Lathom to make out two rows of pews on either side of the singular, central aisle leading to a plain, simple altar.

Lathom stretches, raising his arms fully to the heavens, then seats himself upon a hard bench in the last row. He braces his back for a spasm of pain that doesn't happen.

Grateful for this, he relaxes, yawns from so eventful a day and the late hour, and he breathes deeply—in and out—as Jasmine had tried to teach him a few days earlier, amused that he is following her instruction.

After a dozen such breaths, Lathom's mind clears—for his thoughts are focused on his breath and nothing else—and he feels a surge of... he doesn't know what... a tingling, racing from the toes of his feet through both legs to his spine... then further upward to his brain stem.

A powerful emotion takes hold, from what or where he cannot discern, but can feel his eyes welling with tears until the lower lids can no longer contain them and droplets glide swiftly down both cheeks.

For another few moments—or it could have been minutes—Lathom sits quietly, head bowed.

Finally, he rises to depart.

Outside the chapel, the author strolls back toward Main Street and, turning to absorb the majesty of the snowcapped mountain, sits upon a bench to moon-bathe.

Turning, he fixates on a purple flower called Evening Primrose.

Never in his life has something, anything, looked to him quite so beautiful, so exquisitely perfect. His focus upon it, after a good fifteen seconds, seems to directly connect his consciousness to the flower, to the mystical mountain and sky above. And to all of nature.

Studying the sky now, Lathom focuses his eyes on a maple leaf that has disengaged from its tree and is fluttering, this way and that, slowly, in no particular hurry, without any kind of willfulness or motivation, until it gracefully settles onto the pavement. He further studies the very intricate, organic pattern of reticulation on this blade of foliage, before returning his gaze to the moon, bone white, stunningly bright, its basalt seas and highland mountains richly defined.

It is late, but far from feeling tired, Lathom's euphoria awakens him.

Exultation.

Ataraxy.

And with it, ineffable bliss.

50.

COME morning, Lathom descends the grand staircase to the lobby.

Blythe and Jasmine, sitting at a colonial breakfast table, go quiet.

"Don't let me disturb your conversation," he says, smiling as he helps himself to a mug of joe at the coffee station.

The pair remain silent.

"Mind if I join you?" he asks. He sits down and glances around. "Where's the funeral?"

Blythe and Jasmine exchange a nervous, fleetingly glance.

"Right here," mutters Blythe.

"I spoke again with Aunt Francine," says Jasmine softly. "I told her all about last night, the bookstore in Ashland, how wonderful it all was."

Lathom sips his coffee.

"She wasn't happy," Jasmine continues. "She was especially

unhappy to hear that you are still on board with us. I asked if she would resurrect the bookstore event they'd scheduled in Berkeley…"

"No, no, I don't…"

"She told me to *butt out*. Her exact words. I couldn't believe it. She never talked to me like that before. I've never known my aunt to sound so mean."

"How, may I ask," says Lathom, "does she *normally* sound to you?"

"Well, she never forgets my birthday. Always sends a present. Takes me out shopping when she's in town…"

"Then why is she such a bitch to me?"

Jasmine clams up, as if she's holding something back. "I think she has an issue with *men*," she finally says.

"Oh, one of those," says Lathom.

"One of *those?*" asks Blythe, eyebrow arched.

Jasmine shakes her head. "When my aunt first moved to New York City, after getting her first job in publicity…" she says haltingly. "My aunt was jogging through Central Park. And she got raped."

Silence.

"It gets worse," continues Jasmine. "She called out for help. A couple other guys came to her rescue. Or so she thought. When they saw what was going on, *they* raped her, too." She pauses. "Ever since, she's had a low opinion of men. I think she perceives them all as potential rapists."

Blythe adds, rather abruptly, "She told Jasmine that Mulberry cancelled your book."

"You mean the tour?" says Lathom. "I already know that."

Blythe shakes his head. "No, they cancelled your novel."

"How?" says Lathom, mildly amused. "My novel is already published—and distributed."

Blythe gestures at Jasmine to explain, recuse the middleman.

"She said," says Jasmine, "that because of your conduct and arrest in Seattle, Mulberry Press cancelled your contract and recalled the books they shipped to bookstores. She cited the moral turpitude clause in their contract. And she said you are no longer a Mulberry author."

Lathom takes a long, deep breath, exhales slowly and follows with a sip of coffee.

"Anything else?"

Blythe and Jasmine exchange another glance, this one conveying their mutual sense of incredulity, like, *isn't that enough?*

Neither say anything.

"Okay, then," says Lathom, buoyantly. "What time are we leaving here and where are we going? Or," he chuckles, "am I now stuck here by this mountain with no wheels of my own?"

51.

AFTER four hours and forty minutes, our trio of road-trippers pull into Union Square, smack in the middle of San Francisco.

Jasmine collects her things from the trunk.

"Join us Wednesday—Thanksgiving Eve," she enthuses. "I'll be in North Beach if you're still in town. Big party night."

And off she goes, joyously merging her soul with the city, on her way to practice yoga at Grace Cathedral's open-air labyrinth.

"I guess you've got another seven hour drive ahead of you," says Lathom.

Blythe shakes his head, a defiant glint in his eye. "Nope."

"What do you mean? You've got to get this car back to LA, don't you?"

"No, I don't."

"How's that?"

"I quit."

"Your job?"

"Uh-huh. As of this moment. They can come fetch their damn car. I'm bailing."

"Why?"

"Because of how Mulberry treated you, cancelling your book, leaving you high and dry. And I don't appreciate the way my boss is treating me, either."

"Here's what I'm going to do." Lathom points up. "I'm going to check into this Hyatt Hotel, great location at a decent price. I'll call Amex to cover it and send me a new card. Would you like a room—on me?"

"You sure?"

Lathom nods.

"Okay, thanks. It's not like I have a job anymore—or anything else to do. I'll park this baby for the last time." He chuckles. "Then I'll text Francine and let her know where to have it picked up."

Lathom squints one eye. "You sure you want to do this?"

"Text her?"

"No, quit your job."

"I've never been so sure about anything my whole life."

52.

AROUND five o'clock, Lathom, strolls out of the Hyatt on his own and zigzags northeast toward Chinatown. He passes through Dragon's Gate and wanders up colorful Grant Avenue, in no particular hurry, with no specific destination in mind.

Buddha Bar looks appealing, but the tantalizing aromas from restaurants with barbecued ducks hanging in the window propel him onward, a cocktail less important than satiating a need to eat.

As the author passes a large colorful shop called Canton Bazaar, a musical sound emanating from inside impels him to turn around and retrace his steps, just a few paces. That's where he stops and cocks an ear to listen to the saddest strains of music he's ever heard his whole life. The melody is overwhelming, moving him, again, to tears—an illumination of the senses not unlike his midnight rendezvous with nature's essence beneath Mount Shasta.

Lathom does not know what has swept over him but is experiencing a phenomenon known as adamic ecstasy, having bottomed out.

This wondrous psychological state, oh so powerful, leaves him overcome with joy for no other reason than simply *being*.

He doesn't know what has hit him, only that it feels good, *better* than good, actually quite amazing, and that he needs to cling to it without even wondering why—because, he realizes, the moment he tries to define the feeling it would likely disappear.

The music transcends to another tune and Lathom continues on his way, not bothering to dry his eyes, but surrendering himself absolutely to the cosmos.

Passing Yee's, a Chinatown institution, the aroma of food becomes too much, especially having hardly eaten since breakfast. Despite the nether hour, between lunch and dinner, the restaurant bustles, mostly whole Chinese families sipping tea—and Lathom the only pale face among them.

He goes in planning to order a take-away box—but what's the hurry?

Instead, he seats himself at a plain wooden table and orders barbecue duck and rice.

First, a server places a mug of hot tea without his even asking—the best tea he's ever tasted. And then arrives before him a plate of duck pieces aside a mound of white rice on a bed of Chinese vegetables in oyster sauce.

Lathom thinks he needs a knife, but there isn't one, just a fork, and he notices that everyone around him is using chopsticks, so he struggles to pick up the duck pieces, slowly nibbling at them, fully appreciating their rich flavor (those with crispy skin are the tastiest) and forks the rice and vegetables into his mouth, degusting each new bite.

A veritable feast—*and all (the tea, gratis) for eight bucks?*

Near the top of Grant Avenue, just before Broadway, Lathom's feeling of contentment is accentuated by a realization that he is in familiar territory.

Is that North Beach just around the next corner?

The narrow conduit to Columbus (the grand boulevard that intersects Broadway) is Jack Kerouac Alley, a portal between Eastern and Western culture named after the author of the beat bible, who trolled these very streets looking for wild characters, illuminations—and something strong to drink.

These walls are a swirl of color, graffiti-meets-mural; inside a recessed cavity is a dancing skeleton, symbolic of mortality. *Memento Mori.*

Lathom looks down at the brick walkway and stops at a circular engraving to read a commemoration of Kerouac's words:

The air was soft, the stars so fine, the promise of every cobbled alley so great...

But it is at the end of this colorful path that Lathom finds himself in heaven.

Which is to say, sandwiched between City Lights Bookstore and the iconic Vesuvio Café, where Kerouac, Allen Ginsberg, City Lights co-founder Lawrence Ferlinghetti and the beats drank and partied many a night away—and where a launch party had been thrown for his debut novel a lifetime ago.

He thinks of Wendy. She was there. He shakes his head. If only…

Rounding the corner, while inspecting this shop's funky display windows, Lathom is surprised to see two dozen copies of *Day of the Rabbits* filling a whole center window.

Obviously, the recall ordered by Mulberry was moving in slow motion, just like the book publishing industry in general.

To celebrate this moment, and his short-lived new novel, Lathom enters Vesuvio and sidles up to the front end of the bar, a separate enclave with three stools. He orders Reposado tequila, rocks, a slice of lime and, while awaiting delivery, glances around, absorbing the vibe: a swirl of color, mostly shades of red, gaiety in the galleried space upstairs, piped music courtesy of David Ackles—a song called *Love's Enough*—from *American Gothic*, a lost gem of an LP from the early 1970s.

> *Every time you fall in love.*
> *That's the best time of all.*
> *It's holding sunlight in your hand, it's heaven come to call.*
> *And you wonder: will it last forever?*
> *And you try to keep tomorrow locked away.*
> *'Cos tomorrow is forever*
> *And love's enough for anyone today.*

Lathom experiences another stirring, another illumination,

and, with Kerouac on his mind, conjures up one of Jack's lesser novels, *Satori in Paris*—and experiences what Kerouac had sought.

A young man sitting at the main bar nearby, who'd been observing the older gentleman savor his libation, finally speaks.

"Aren't you Christopher Lathom, the author?"

Lathom stiffens—*another process server?*

He is noncommittal, says nothing.

"Congratulations on your new novel, sir," the stranger continues. "I just read it—and loved every page. I doff my hat to you." And, indeed, he doffs his black pork-pie.

Lathom toasts the air. "Thank you, my friend. Hearing somebody say that means more to me than anything— certainly more than what the literary snob brigade writes in their journals."

"May I buy you a drink?"

Lathom shrugs. "Why not?" He is feeling whimsical— happy this wasn't another invitation to the judicial system and, paraphrasing young Jasmine, "Tonight, I'm open to whatever the universe has in store for me."

The young man, clad in a black turtleneck sweater, skinny black jeans, Chelsea boots and thick black-rimmed glasses, smiles. "I like that," he says, sliding off his barstool to sit nearer Lathom. "What brings you to Baghdad-by-the-Bay? A book tour?"

Lathom chuckles. "That's what *got* me here." He pauses to take a gulp of tequila.

"But it's over now."

"That's a shame," says the young man. "Too bad you're not here to sign books across the alley."

Lathom brightens. "That's what I thought. My favorite bookstore in the world. But too late now."

"Why's that?"

"My publisher just cancelled it."

"The tour?"

"No, the *book*." He gestures out the door toward the famed bookstore. "I'm surprised to see copies in their window."

The young man seems totally baffled. "I don't understand. Why was it cancelled?"

"I don't know if you heard, but I got hauled into court a few days ago for patting a woman's butt."

"So what?" he says. "The *Me-Too* movement's gone nuts. What does that have to do with *literature?*"

Lathom shakes his head. "Beats the hell out of me. But none of it matters anymore. Just being here, right now..." he pauses. "I think I'm exactly where I'm supposed to be."

"I'm in no doubt that you're right," says the young man. "My name is Oskatel." He offers his right hand.

Lathom hesitates a moment, knuckles him. "I'm getting over an ear infection," he explains. "Don't want to spread my germs."

"No worries." Oskatel pauses. "I'm the editorial director at a new imprint called Illuminated Minds. We're supported by a large publishing house in the Big Apple with great distribution. And I have a proposition for you."

53.

WALKING back through Chinatown, Lathom checks his phone for the first time since switching it off before his moonlit stroll in McCloud the night before. Powering it while strolling adjacent to Old St. Mary's Cathedral, he looks up at the clock tower. Time matters not, at this point of his journey, but the inscription below the round clock speaks to him as if it were a message from the cosmos:

Son, observe the time and fly from evil.

The several messages awaiting his attention are from Jason Downey, his agent—including a text: *Phone me urgent.*

It is midevening in New York City but Downey answers while dining in a fancy restaurant, having just attended a book reception for one of his up-and-coming ethnic authors.

"Is my book canceled?" Lathom preempts his agent.

"Unfortunately, it is. Where are you?"

"So, it's official?"

"Very."

"Marvelous!"

"Excuse me?"

"You're excused. Bye."

"Wait—don't go!"

But Lathom has already disconnected his agent. Forever. And powered off his phone.

Approaching his hotel, Lathom decides to continue his stroll, all the way down to Union Square where an eighty-three-foot fir tree is in the midst of being prepped for decoration and ceremonial illumination the day after Thanksgiving when retailers thankfully expect the hordes to color their Friday black.

In the distance, Lathom barely makes out Blythe, who has his back to him, staring out at the ice skating rink, empty and quiet aside from the hum of an ice resurfacer.

He crosses Post Street and settles a few yards behind his former media escort.

Blythe senses the presence of another and turns around.

Their eyes connect.

"I'm proud of you, Blythe." Lathom steps forward to his grandson. "I'm glad you accidentally made yourself known to me," he says, hugging him. "I always wanted a son. I'm sorry he's not here. But he's given me something better."

He cannot see the tears welling in his grandson's eyes.

"I'm planning to stay through Thursday," says Lathom. "I'll cover the cost of your room if you want to stay on with me."

"Really?"

Lathom nods. "Least I can do, considering I've missed twenty-two of your birthdays." He looks around. "C'mon, let's go get a bowl of the world's best cioppino at Tadich."

54.

Next morning, seeing the world with fresh eyes—fresher than ever before—Christopher Lathom watches the hustle and bustle on the corner of Stockton and Sutter Streets over coffee inside Starbucks and hatches a new plan, which he springs on his grandson when Blythe eventually appears, late, having suffered food coma from feasting the evening before.

"We're moving upmarket." Lathom announces. "Mark Hopkins. I found a patron."

Blythe sips his coffee. "Who's Mark Hopkins?"

"Mark Hopkins isn't a person. It's a hotel, on Nob Hill, not far from here. Part of the Intercontinental chain."

"Sounds pricey," says Blythe, shaking his head. "I can't afford that."

"You don't have to, remember? I'm affording it."

"How?"

"That's where the patron comes in—propitiously."

And so, mid-afternoon, as the fog begins to roll into the bay area from the ocean, casting a fogbow from heaven to earth and high winds thrash the highest point of the city, Lathom checks Blythe and himself into swankier digs: an historic landmark featuring plush rooms with windows that still open.

Delicately, Lathom picks up the TV remote in his room and powers it on. And for the next ten minutes he patiently works his way through programming until he has it completely mastered.

55.

In the shadow of Grace Cathedral whose French Gothic architecture and twin towers makes it a dead ringer for Notre Dame in Paris, Lathom guides Blythe into The Big 4 (so named after California's Big Four railroad magnates), an old-worldly restaurant and bar within Huntington Hotel, between the cathedral and their own new digs.

The bar's mahogany-paneled walls and hunter green seat coverings and incandescent table lamps give it the feel and texture of a nineteenth century gentlemen's club.

The two men are guided to a booth adjacent to the bar, reserved earlier by their hotel concierge at Lathom's request, to the accompaniment of "Being Alive" from the stage-show *Company*, courtesy of a female pianist, who taps the ebonies and ivories with dramatic flair.

A server appears to take their order.

"I think I'm up for an evening prayer," says Lathom,

surveying the cocktail list. "Which means I'll try your Vesper."

"What's that?" asks Blythe.

"If they do it right, heaven in a glass," says Lathom. "Two parts gin, one part vodka, half-part Lillet and a twist."

Blythe nods. "Make it two—no car to drive!"

Lathom is quiet, awaiting his prayer, looking around.

"Hasn't changed much," he comments.

"When were you last here?"

Lathom breathes deeply, exhaling with a sigh. "The evening of the day a check arrived, the advance for my first novel." He pauses. "My typewritten manuscript had been roundly rejected by the obligatory two-dozen publishers. I was about to give up writing. I put my manuscript in the trash. Without my knowing, your grandmother retrieved it from the garbage can outside our Sausalito houseboat and sent it—the only copy—to a publisher she thought might like it."

A pair of Vespers arrive.

"What happened next?" Blythe is greatly intrigued.

"A couple months after I thought the manuscript was gone forever—no carbon copy, nothing—I was kicking myself for being so rash and tossing it out. Then out of the blue I receive a letter from a publisher saying they want to publish my novel. I couldn't believe my eyes, because, of course, it was a publisher I'd never sent it to. Wendy, your grandmother, fessed up and told me what she'd done. Next thing, they sent an advance check—more money than I'd ever had to my name."

Lathom catches his breath before continuing.

"So, I took your grandmother out to celebrate. We rode a bus from Sausalito into the big city. And this place..." he gestures widely with both arms. "The Big 4, is where we came for drinks and dinner." He pauses.

"And that was the first and only time I've been here. Until this evening." He looks around. "I'm happy to report that unlike everything else in the world, this place has not changed one iota."

The pianist, whose obvious specialty is classic show-tunes, graciously segues into "I Dreamed a Dream" from *Les Miserables*.

Blythe remains silent as Lathom continues.

"Without me knowing, your grandmother went out and bought me a present and gave it to me right here, at this very table. I think she must have hocked the diamond ring she inherited from her mother to buy it."

From his left wrist Lathom unclasps a round-faced gold timepiece and places it on the table.

"Patek Philippe," he says, pushing it across the surface toward Blythe. "It's the only thing I've ever owned worth a damn. And it's a not a quartz zombie, so you'll have to wind it."

"Huh?"

"It's yours, take it."

"No, no—I couldn't."

"If you don't take it, it's staying on this table after we leave."

"Why?"

"I don't want it anymore. *You* should have it. It came from *your* grandmother. Consider it a family heirloom—a handsel to you, the rightful owner."

"Handsel?"

"Better get cracking on that vocabulary book I gave you. A handsel is a gift at the start of something new—in this case, a new relationship between grandfather and grandson."

"But don't you need it?"

Lathom shakes his head, "I don't give a damn about time anymore. And I never cared much for personal possessions. Invite them into your life and they try to own you."

Blythe picks up the precious wristwatch. "I've never worn a watch," he says softly. "But I'll wear this one. Always." He puts the timepiece to his ear and listens to its faint ticking for a few seconds before buckling the black alligator strap around his wrist. Then he looks up into his grandfather's eyes.

"Let's not get all lachrymose," says Lathom, his voice trembling just a tad, "but I still love her."

Blythe looks at him, a quizzical expression.

"Your grandmother. I still love her."

Blythe reaches into the inside pocket of his sport coat and retrieves a small silver square, aged from the look of its dark patina.

He opens it to a pair of black-and-white photo booth pics—and passes it to Lathom.

"It was my father's," Blythe explains. "Since we're exchanging gifts."

In the left frame, a photo of Wendy, flashing a big smile; on the right, a young man and a little boy.

Lathom's eyes rotate back and forth between the two old photos.

"Me and my dad," Blythe adds. "It was one of the personal effects the army sent back from Afghanistan. They told us he always carried it on him."

Lathom is mesmerized by the image, never seen before this moment, recognizing that his son is the spitting image of himself as a young man.

Unable to arrest a surge of emotion through his very soul, Lathom abruptly excuses himself, barely finding his way to the men's room through tear-filled eyes.

After pushing the door open, locking himself inside, Lathom loses the composure he'd been trying to maintain his whole life, breaking down into a bundle of uncontrollable sobs.

PART FIVE

56.

WEDNESDAY evening.

Thanksgiving Eve.

City Lights Bookstore.

The shop display windows—all of them—feature, exclusively, *Day of the Rabbits* by Christopher Lathom.

Several large posters announce a special, hastily put together book event commencing at six o'clock, featuring the author himself to discuss his new novel and to sign copies.

Lathom and Blythe arrive together looking ultra-sharp, having spent a few hours earlier in the day at Cable Car Clothiers on Sutter Street to attire themselves in classic wear from head to toe, including rabbit felt fedoras from Lock & Co in England, add suede monk strap shoes from The Alden Shop a few doors down.

The book bash upstairs in the bookstore's Poetry &

Beats Room is in full swing, with scores of revelers drinking sparkling wine from glass flutes, when Jasmine and members of her family—including Aunt Francine, who had unexpectedly flown in for Thanksgiving—wander past on their way to Chinatown.

Jasmine notices it first: a poster, Lathom's books in the window—and much bustle inside.

She stops short, her face beaming with a smile that lights up the North Beach night.

Francine Fassbender, behind her, does a double-take, then freezes in her tracks, mortified by what she sees. Her next emotion is anger—and it launches her, full throttle, into the bookstore, exuding thunder and lighting.

"Who's in charge here?" she snaps at the hip young male behind a counter near the entrance.

He motions her with his head toward the next room.

Francine journeys further into this rabbit warren of a bookstore until she reaches the last room, then left, up a steep wooden staircase. There, she sees a rather cleaned-up Christopher Lathom holding court with a bevy of admirers.

Her eyes are bugging by the time she reaches Oskatel, clearly the master of ceremonies, and she plants herself directly in front of him.

"What the devil is going on here?" she demands.

The editorial director of Illuminated Minds is nonplussed, and somewhat amused, having no idea who this obnoxious person might be.

"We call this an author event," he deadpans.

"But... but... this book was *cancelled!*"

Oskatel looks around at the roomful of books and people. "Doesn't look like that to me," he says.

"We have books. We have an author. And we have customers. Actually, that makes it a trifecta for a book-signing event."

"But you don't have a *publisher!*" shrills Francine. "I am a senior executive at Mulberry Press and *I personally cancelled this book!*"

"Ah, yes, Francine Fassbender. Why, hello, I've heard about you. Apparently, City Lights ordered a good many books, though I fear they will sell out this evening."

Francine looks around, incredulous. "But this is ridiculous! They won't get any more."

"On the contrary, madam. Illuminated Minds just inked an agreement with the sales manager at Mulberry Press to purchase your remaining stock of books while we prepare our own print run."

"Excuse me?"

"We heard that the author's contract with Mulberry was terminated and thus we were able to enter into an agreement with Mister Lathom. We are the new and very proud publisher of *Day of the Rabbi*ts. And please accept my personal thanks for delivering him to us. As publishers of literary works, we rarely have a large commercial success—though I expect we will with this outstanding novel."

Francine, apoplectic with rage by now, does not know what to say—and her anger compounds exponentially when she observes Blythe standing nearby, smiling and sipping bubbly.

She stomps over and confronts him. "How dare you quit in the middle of a book tour!"

Blythe, who had only a moment earlier been looking at *The Book of Donkeys*, nervously expounds, involuntarily, a series of donkey-like *hee-haws* at a rather high pitch, leaving his ex-boss baffled and vastly more perplexed than before.

"I've reported the car you were driving stolen!" she shrills.

"I hope not, for your sake," says Blythe. "I can prove I sent you a text and e-mail saying the valet at the Hyatt Hotel has your car-park ticket. Filing a false police report is a crime."

Francine seethes, turns her back on Blythe, and aims herself at Lathom, the effulgent star of tonight's show and the true object of her anger, besieged as he is these moments by adoring fans.

"I will ruin you!" she hollers.

Lathom smiles graciously. "I forgive you, Francine."

"*You* forgive *me?*"

"Like the fragrance of a violet crushed by your heel."

"What?"

"Mark Twain. If you're going to work in publishing, I suggest you read a few classics. Oh, and thank you for inserting your sagacious niece, Jasmine, into our book drive. You should spend more time with her yourself rather than pawning her off on others—she's an inspiration."

Contorting her face, Francine turns on her high-heels and stomps out, loudly, on the slatted wooden floor, almost toppling down the steep staircase. For the best comeuppance of all is forgiveness.

In her place, Jasmine appears at the top of the stairs.

Lathom excuses himself and glides over, plants a gentle kiss on her forehead.

"Assuming this is truly you," he whispers, "thanks for everything."

Jasmine grins. "Feeling somewhat transformed?"

Lathom nods. "Apotheosis."

Jasmine smiles broadly. "Remember, before enlightenment, chop wood, carry water," she says. "After enlightenment, chop wood, carry water. And," she adds with a wink, "don't tell anyone."

57.

It transpired that Lathom's new publisher, Illuminated Minds, had once been targeted by Heinrich Schmucker, the same sewer-vexatious litigant suing Lathom for so-called copy infringement.

Despite significant legal expense, Illuminated Minds had refused to give into Schmucker's extortionate nonsense and settle the dispute. They had fought it all the way to trial, on the eve of which the court dismissed the case, with prejudice, for lack of merit.

So now, as part of Lathom's publishing contract, Illuminated Minds agreed, at its own cost, to use the very same lawyer—on perpetual retainer to them—for aggressively defending their author's innocence and reputation as part of an overall program to update and improve Lathom's profile on all digital platforms, including Amazon.

To that end, the publisher hired its own photographer to snap their new author's portrait.

Confronted by his former nemesis, a formidable legal adversary with experience dealing it back to him for a frivolous copyright infringement claims, shakedown artist Schmucker folded his hand.

But Schmucker's troubles did not end there.

A private investigator hired by legal counsel for Illuminated Minds discovered the conman had falsified copyright registration, rendering it invalid.

Thus, a countersuit was filed against Schmucker for malicious prosecution, fraud and deceit. And the hapless hustler was eventually held liable for all of Lathom's legal fees.

58.

THANKSGIVING Day.

The city is quiet and deserted.

The day before, nine days since launching on his book tour from Montecito, Lathom (no driver's license, he) rented (for Blythe to drive) a Chevy Blazer with this plan: blaze off, the day after everyone else from Fog City had departed.

Blythe readjusts his rearview mirror and tackles the interchange for 101 South.

"Are you really gay?" asks Lathom.

"I am."

"Why?"

"I don't know why. I only know that I am."

"Are you happy?"

"Am I *happy*?"

"I mean, the way you are."

"The way I am? You mean gay?"

"Yes."

Blythe shrugs. "I'm happy, generally. I don't know if my gayness has anything to do with it, with being happy. I just am. But if you're asking, am I comfortable in my own skin…"

"I guess that's what I'm asking."

"For me, it's the most natural thing in the world."

"Do you think it had anything to do with your upbringing?" asks Lathom.

"Being gay?"

"Uh-huh."

"You mean growing up without a father figure around?"

"I guess that's what I mean."

"I used to think about that." Blythe shakes his head. "No." He shrugs. "It's just who I am, what I am."

"And your grandmother?"

"And my grandmother, what?"

"She knows?"

"That I'm gay? Of course."

"And she was okay with it?"

"Grandma Wendy had no hesitation accepting who I am." A few seconds pass. "What about you?"

Lathom takes a few seconds. "As long as you're happy, I'm okay with whatever you choose to be."

"Just okay?"

"You have to understand, it's harder for me to move with the trends of my time because, as a writer, I've always been an outsider looking in, instead of being part of the flow. But I'm thinking this road trip has helped improve my perspective."

"I have a question for you," says Blythe.

"Shoot."

"Why did it take so long for you to write your second novel?"

"Didn't take me long to write," says Lathom. "But it took many years for me to be *satisfied* with it."

"Thirty years?"

"Time flies," says Lathom. "And manuscripts need to breathe. Sometimes I'd let a whole year go by without taking a peek."

"Why?"

"Simple: so that I could see its glaring errors with fresh eyes." He pauses. "But let's say you still want to write, even after experiencing this book tour from hell."

"I do. More than ever."

"There's three edits you must always do—and you're not allowed to do them until you've revised your writing so much there isn't one thing you'd change. Or so you believe at the time."

"I'm listening."

"One, print out your manuscript. Don't rely on the computer screen to assess what you've written. You'd be surprised how different everything looks on paper. No page will come out unscathed by multiple edits.

"Two, read it aloud to yourself. The rhythm must be perfect and dialogue has to sound natural, like someone— your characters—are truly speaking it.

"Three—and you can do this before one and two—do a *random* edit."

"A what?"

"Don't read your manuscript from beginning to end. Jump in at a random page."

"Why?"

"So that your attention is focused not on how the story unfolds, but on the words, phrases and sentences, separated from the storyline. Each and every word—the *right* word—must have a reason for taking up space. Choose a number between one and nine, could be the day of the month. Say it's the 29th. Nine is your number. Skip to every page that has a nine in it. And so on. Until the whole manuscript has been randomly edited.

"Finally, try an edit under the influence."

"Under the influence of what?"

"Booze. Pot, if that's your thing. See how it reads, how it sounds. You're trying to look at your writing from every angle you possibly can. And any edits you make under-the-influence, double-check later. Half, you'll keep, the other half you'll disregard and revert to the original.

"And by the time you think you're finished, which you're probably not, you're so sick of looking at it, of reading it, that you'd love to throw it onto a bonfire."

59.

Two hours into the drive, just past Prunedale, Lathom points to an exit sign for Route 156. "Let's get off here."

"You need to use the john?"

"No. If memory serves me correct, 156 will turn into Route 1, Pacific Coast Highway, and that should take us to the Monterey Peninsula."

"You want to take the long way for some scenery?" Blythe ramps off in a westerly direction.

"Not exactly."

***

As navigated by Lathom, Blythe slides the car into a space on the curb outside a modest ranch house a few blocks from Monterey's commercial zone.

"Okay," says Blythe. "There must be a reason for this. What next?"

"Would you like to meet my daughter—your aunt?"

"She invited you for Thanksgiving?"

Lathom shakes his head, a mischievous grin. "She and I haven't spoken in seven or eight years."

"So she's not expecting you."

"Definitely not."

Now it is Blythe's turn to grin.

"This definitely has potential."

"Don't know about that," says Lathom. "But what's Thanksgiving without a little family drama?"

He reaches for the door handle.

"Wait," says Blythe. "We can't just show up empty-handed."

Lathom, never the brightest lamp on the street with regard to social skills, nods. "You're right. I'm glad you were brought up better than I was."

He looks straight ahead, his mind's eye focused inward. "I doubt you know this, but my mother, bless her soul, lost her husband—my father—to World War Two. Things got so bad, she had to turn to prostitution for the money she needed to feed her kid—me."

He sighs, considering whether or not to continue. "Once, when I was small, one of her johns whacked me across the face and I tumbled down a stairway."

He pauses, wincing, and looks ahead vacantly, then turns back to face Blythe. "Never got over it. If I seem angry sometimes, well, now you know why. It's always been me against the world."

Blythe digests this in silence, then asks, "Thanks for sharing."

"There must be a Starbucks somewhere around here," says Lathom. "There always is. And they're always open."

Blythe accesses the Internet on his phone. "Nearest is Del Monte—a couple blocks from here."

And indeed, just a few minutes later, Lathom assembles a makeshift gift box of ground beans, chocolate covered almonds and madeleine cookies, along with paper cups of coffee for the road.

And soon they are back in the same residential parking space as before.

"Okay," says Lathom, unsure what to expect. "I should go first."

He climbs out, gathers himself and his gift and trudges up the paved, uneven walkway toward the front door, looking back at Blythe, a quick wink, before sucking in a lungful of fresh air and pressing the doorbell.

The door creaks open a few inches, then widens, along with the eyes of a woman wearing an apron who is shocked by what she sees standing before her.

"What the heck are *you* doing here?"

Yup, Lathom realizes, same person at the coffee stop in Soledad—what, a week ago? *And what a week!*

"It's Thanksgiving," says Lathom. "Thought I'd pop by. Here, I have something for you." He offers the Starbucks box.

His daughter ignores it. "You thought you'd *pop by?*"

Lathom shrugs. "On my way back from San Francisco. I've been on a book tour."

"Yeah, I saw something about that on the news. You're looking for a place to hide, right?"

Lathom shakes his head. "Wrong."

"Money?"

"No."

"But you think I'm supposed to invite you in?"

"I come with no expectations. Someone who joined me for part of the trip taught me that part of the key to happiness is low expectations."

A mocha-skinned little girl about three years-young appears, tugging at the woman's leg. "Mama, who's that?"

She looks down. "No one."

"Yup, that's me," says Lathom. "Mister No One. I should probably leave." He turns and almost bumps into Blythe, who has come up briskly from behind.

"Hello," says Blythe to the woman behind the door.

She looks at him in surprise.

"Who the hell are you?"

Blythe chuckles. "Like father, like daughter." He glances at his aunt, then his grandfather, and again at his aunt, settling his eyes into hers. "I'm your dad's grandson."

60.

Blythe and Lathom are reseated in the Chevy Blazer, ready to roll, when a man, somewhere in age between the two, scurries from the house and waves them down.

"Sorry about my wife's harsh words," says the trim clean-shaven and very smiley African-American. "Holidays are a stressful time. But I talked to her. It's Thanksgiving, a time for family, no matter the circumstances. Please come inside and feel welcome in our home. I'd like you to meet your granddaughter."

Lathom nods, trying to keep his emotions in check by so gracious an invitation and, more significantly, the discovery of having not just one but *two* grandchildren.

Slowly, he climbs out and, with Blythe behind him, trudges up the path alongside his son-in-law who, almost at the front door, turns and says, "I've been waiting a long time for your second novel."

Lathom stops in his tracks and brightens.

"Really?"

The man nods. "Been a huge fan forever. And I've been waiting a long time for you to show up here. Glad you finally arrived."

Just inside the front door, the little girl he'd met a few minutes earlier practically blocks Lathom's way, looking straight up at him.

"Are you my gran' pa?" she asks, wide-eyed with suspicion.

Lathom sits down, cross-legged, so he can look directly into her eyes. "Seems like I'm *everybody's* gran' pa," he says. "But, yes, young lady—I'm Papa Chris. It is my very great pleasure to finally meet you." He smiles. "I bet you've never seen a bearded dragon?"

She shakes her head.

"Would you like to?"

She glances at her dad for reassurance then resumes her gaze on *gran' pa*. "Uh-huh."

Lathom rises. "Come." He reaches for her hand. "I'll introduce you to Scallywag."

"Scallywag?"

Lathom nods. "That's his name. It's what my mother called *me* when I was your age."

61.

TEN minutes later, Lathom and his daughter, just the two of them, sit upon stools at an island in the kitchen, facing one another, the aroma of a turkey basting in the oven.

She asks, "Am I supposed to be happy about this?"

He replies, "Only you can choose whether or not to be happy about anything. But the only way you'll find happiness is acceptance of whatever the situation is around you. Everyone bears a cross of some kind. It's a willingness to accept those things over which we have no control that makes all things in life bearable. How's your mother?" he adds.

"Are you asking because you're really interested?"

Lathom considers this and replies thoughtfully. "I think I saw you at Starbucks in Soledad about a week ago. If we had spoken then, I probably wouldn't have asked about her. But much has happened since, so, yes, I am interested."

His daughter digests this.

"Getting arrested for sexual assault changed you?"

Lathom chuckles, shaking his head.

"There's much more to it than that."

He pauses.

"I have no idea whether I'm supposed to forgive you or you're supposed to forgive me," Lathom continues, "though I suspect it's the latter, given my propensity for being difficult, an unhealthy disposition I'm finally doing something about. If I have wronged you in any way—and I assume I have—I ask your forgiveness. Because you are family, you're all I really have—except for Scallywag, my bearded dragon."

He places his hand over hers.

"And I love you."

A tear slips down his daughter's left cheek.

She reaches out and takes his hand.

"I love you too, Dad."

62.

"I have an admission," says Blythe, a sheepish smirk crossing his face, eyes fixed upon the road ahead.

Post-Thanksgiving dinner, he and Lathom are driving to Cannery Row on Monterey's waterfront to find a hotel for the night.

Lathom does not respond and Blythe eventually fills the silence. "It's about my grandmother."

"Oh?" says Lathom, mellow from a tummy full of tryptophan and trimmings. "What about her?"

Blythe takes a moment. "I lied about her being gone." He glances furtively at his passenger.

"About being gone?"

"My grandmother is still alive."

Lathom takes a few long seconds to digest this new twist.

"I'm sorry I...," Blythe adds.

"No, no." Lathom smiles. "I'm *happy* Wendy is alive."

"But I need to explain myself." Blythe bows his head. "My grandmother knew what I was planning to do, becoming your media escort and trying to get to know you. She didn't encourage me. But she didn't try to stop me either. She's like that, never controlling in any way. She also knew that I had no intention of revealing my true identity to you."

He takes a breath. "So, when you found out by accident, I felt I needed to keep her out of it, to protect her from my recklessness. Even though it meant lying."

He pauses. "But now that I know how much you cared for her, how much she meant to you..." he lowers his voice, trembling with emotion. "And that you still love her..." he trails off. "It would be wrong of me to let you keep believing she's gone forever."

He pauses. "I had to set it straight."

The silence in the car is broken by the jingling of Blythe's smart phone, placed upon the console between himself and Lathom.

Blythe glances down and sees the caller's identity.

Grandma.

He glances over at Lathom, who sees it too.

"You answer it," says Blythe.

"Your idea of denouement?"

Blythe nods.

"I think she might like to hear your voice again."

EPILOGUE

THE Prosecuting Attorney's Office in Seattle declined to proceed with a sexual assault complaint against Christopher Lathom after discovering that the alleged victim had filed three such claims over the past two years; only one had gone to trial, resulting in acquittal.

Case dismissed.

As reissued, marketed and promoted by Illuminated Minds, *The Day of the Rabbits* became a *New York Times* and Amazon bestseller.

Mulberry Press fired Francine as publicity chief, not for losing out on the success of Christopher Lathom's long-awaited novel, but paying for the hotel bills of a family member on the company's dime.

Instead of taking up residence at Abbey Shasta monastery, Jasmine journeyed to India, lived on an ashram and, camping atop the Himalayas, successfully crossed the razor's edge.

Upon her return, Jasmine settled into the wine valley of Santa Ynez and opened an inn where she shared, in passing, her spiritual vision, impacting positively upon guests and changing very many lives for the better.

I see her from time to time.

In fact, when I, Blythe Lathom, published my first novel, we had a party in the restaurant of her inn to celebrate the publication of my book.

And to ceremonialize the wedding of my grandparents— Christopher and Wendy—as foreshadowed by Jasmine's *feast-forward* in Ashland, Oregon.

The day after, I embarked on my own tour to promote... *Book Drive*.